C000020302

SMAILHOLM

BOOK ONE

SMAILHOLM

C.L. Williams

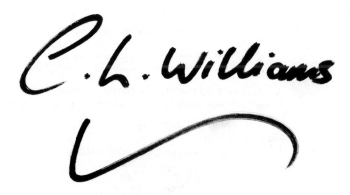

Copyright © 2020 C. L. Williams

The moral right of the author has been asserted.

Illustrations © David Rolls
Cover Design by Holly Dunn
Map Design by Joshua Stolarz
Author Photo by Helen Walsh

Apart from any fair dealing for the purposes of research or private study,
or criticism or review, as permitted under the Copyright, Designs and Patents
Act 1988, this publication may only be reproduced, stored or transmitted, in
any form or by any means, with the prior permission in writing of the
publishers, or in the case of reprographic reproduction in accordance with
the terms of licences issued by the Copyright Licensing Agency. Enquiries
concerning reproduction outside those terms should be sent to the publishers.

Matador
9 Priory Business Park,
Wistow Road, Kibworth Beauchamp,
Leicestershire LE8 0RX
Tel: 0116 279 2299
Email: books@troubador.co.uk
Web: www.troubador.co.uk/matador
Twitter: @matadorbooks

ISBN 978 1838591 656

British Library Cataloguing in Publication Data.
A catalogue record for this book is available from the British Library.

Printed and bound by CPI Group (UK) Ltd, Croydon, CR0 4YY
Typeset in 11pt Adobe Jenson Pro by Troubador Publishing Ltd, Leicester, UK

❡

Matador is an imprint of Troubador Publishing Ltd

MIX
Paper from
responsible sources
FSC
www.fsc.org   FSC® C013604

For Ava and Henry

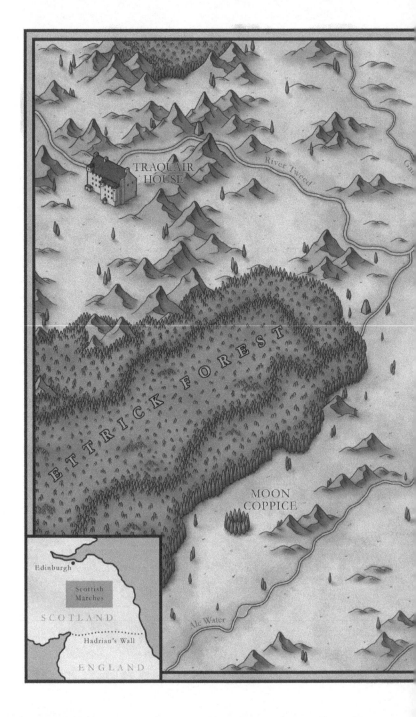

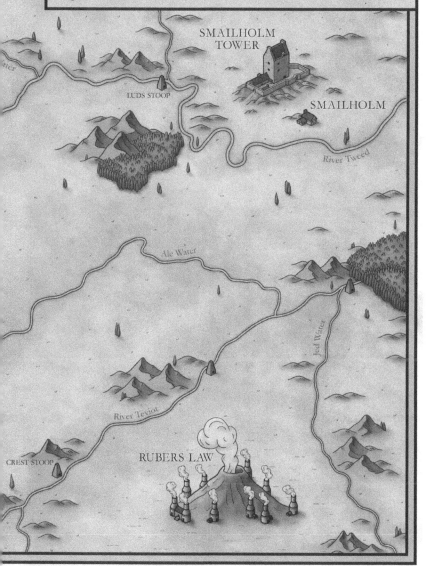

For those who seek adventure away from this place,
Let it be so—always.
Remember though, to look behind you from whence you came,
lest you forget what you might have had if you had stayed,
or turned in another direction.

CHAPTER ONE

Smailholm Tower 1565

I n the great Tower's shadow the river weaves down to a rocky outcrop covered in brambles—deep purple and green as ever has been known in the late August sun. Here, beneath the flowers of late summer, something is stirring. Quickly I find my favourite spot and lean forwards, carefully placing my ear above the brambles. Prickly thorns scratch against my cheek; the scent of recent raindrops fresh and heady filling my nostrils. The sunlight shines bright in my eyes and I squint to the horizon to check I've not been followed.

I crouch down behind the rocks, my hands brushing against a blanket of soft green moss. Finally, I am out of sight of the Tower. The noise of my own breath, so loud about my ears, crowds out all other sound. 'Shh, calm yourself,' I whisper.

Placing my hand over my mouth to stifle my heavy breaths, I lean in even closer, so that my face is completely covered by the brambles and my hands claw at the sodden earth beneath.

It is the sound I hear first, surprising me as it always has done. It seems so strange, with no one around, to hear the noise of a busy village in an otherwise silent place. Horses hooves clip against the cobbles that pepper the muddy earth, as the pocket-sized folk make their way into Smailholm's miniature marketplace.

It is busy today and I wonder what has brought more visitors into the village. Mrs Jetty, the baker's wife, seems merrier than usual—no doubt pleased at the extra custom. Announcing she is open for trade, she sings a cheerful melody.

Baking since dawn,
Whilst Smailholm yawns,
Quick from the oven,
A baker's dozen'

Despite how tiny she might seem; her voice, which is pitched low, echoes up to my ears perfectly. She is every bit as you would expect of a baker's wife; her ample waist bursting her apron seams and cheeks red with effort from hard work at the stove. Every bit as you would expect that is, except for her size. For compared to me, she is no bigger than one of my peg dolls. So tiny she is, I could pick her up in the palm of my hand, put her in my pocket and you wouldn't think she was there at all. She has no wings to make her fly; nor ears that point to a peak. She is neither a fairy nor a spritely elf, as the old folk tales might say. Simply a jolly woman singing a jolly song. In fact, if my size didn't dwarf her tiny frame you wouldn't realise she was any different at all.

This place Mrs Jetty calls home is just like any other village, with its inn, stables, church and some ten houses dotted around a central water well. All so perfectly formed, yet in miniature with tiny leaded windows, doors and chimneys where now the grey smoke rises and tickles the back of my nose, making me sneeze. The tiny horses in the stable below neigh at my noisy intrusion and kick their legs at the doors in protest.

Closing my eyes, I smell the soot of burning coals as Caen the blacksmith bangs, turns and moulds his molten metal. The shrill sound of metal against metal startles me and I open my eyes to see another visitor enter the marketplace. One that I know better than any other—my dearest friend Jimmy. Even though he is so tiny to my eyes, I can still make out the beads of sweat that trickle down his brow, dampening his messy white blond hair at the tips. His turquoise blue eyes glisten in the sun and his cheeks carry a rosy blush. His neck is taut from the effort of pulling water from the well and he mops the sweat from his brow with the sleeve of his loose white shirt. Untucked from his simple linen breeches, his shirt billows in the breeze, loose at the sleeves yet clinging slightly to his torso. Clanging the pail of water down in exhaustion he finally looks up at my giant-like form. After all, to Smailholm folk I'm hard to miss.

'Morning lass, I thought you were busy today with your uncle, visiting 'n' all,' he says, shading his eyes with his hand from the glare of the sun to look up at me, as if nothing is amiss. How can it be that these tiniest of folk don't even blink when they see a giant like I, peering down into their tiny world?

'I'm avoiding it, nay dreading it,' I reply, as I always do, in a whisper. My voice, at normal volume, is hundreds of times louder than theirs, and must sometimes hurt their tiny ears. Yet other than my hushed conversation with Jimmy, life goes on in Smailholm just as it always has. The presence of the giant girl ignored.

You see for many years a secret has been kept beneath my family home—Smailholm Tower, the wild brambles hiding a big secret of the smallest kind. It is a secret which only I seem to have discovered—that of the miniature folk of Smailholm. They say they were once the same size as I, but they were shrunk by some other-worldly curse.

When Jimmy first told me tales of a faceless sorceress casting a curse on all those who lived beneath Smailholm Tower my ears burned hot, yet my body chilled cold. Why would any of my clan be banished to live beneath these thick brambles? Such curses always seem a little hard to believe until you see them for yourself. Even though such tiny folk are regularly before my very eyes, I cannot imagine what cruelness could have made them so. Besides, I hope in my heart that there's no such beings as witches or faceless sorceresses. Whilst my nightmares are often plagued by such creatures they have no place in Smailholm on this fine sunny day.

'I know what you mean, we too have unsettling news today. Laird Falmouth has called a meeting of all in the village,' Jimmy says, suddenly interrupting my thoughts. 'I don't know how he dares order us about, for he's not to be seen here most of the time. Off on some frivolous pursuit. Hunting he calls it, but I've never seen him bring much meat back of any kind. He's too busy lying under an oak tree in Ettrick lamenting his small place in the world.

'If it weren't for my sister and I hunting and farming the land I dread to think what we would eat. Some Laird of Smailholm he calls himself!'

'Do you know what the meeting is about?' I ask.

'Aye lass. Some worry about Smailholm being discovered. There are rumours that he's prepared to take a hunting party out to find a cure for our strange predicament.'

'Oh Jimmy, what unexpected news this day brings,' I say, bubbles of excitement popping in my tummy. 'Just imagine how different it would be if we were to be the same size!'

'Hmm. I'm not so sure lass. We've been happy enough, haven't we? Just look around at this place,' Jimmy says, his hand gesturing towards the miniature stalls and folk bustling about the marketplace. Indeed, there appears nothing strange or unhappy to be found in this tiny world. As the sun warms my back and the smell of fresh bread still wafts up my nose, making my mouth water at the very thought of it, I wonder too if anything at all should change. For small or large Smailholm will always be my favourite place.

'I don't see many wishing it could be different. Seems to me we are just right as we are,' Jimmy says, 'after all most folk here don't know any different. The last of our men to know a normal-sized world have died—along with any great desire to reverse the curse. In fact, it was Laird Falmouth's father himself who was the last to know both sized worlds, and who urged, with his last breath, his son seek a cure to our tiny size. A quest that seemed to be peacefully unheeded, until now at least. What change it will now heap upon this place I dare not think,' he says, his brow wrinkling with lines of worry. 'I, for one, am happy with my place in this world, tiny though it may be.'

Jimmy may only be fifteen, yet his shoulders, despite their broadness earned from farming the land, seem to have the weight of his tiny world upon them. I can always tell when he worries; his eyes show every little thing he's feeling. It is quite unusual for a girl to have a boy best friend, particularly when the boy is so miniature in size to her own—yet Jimmy really is just that. My best friend. Since we met two years ago now, when I first peered down between the brambles to look in startlement upon his fair face, we've spent nearly every day together. Summers have come and gone, Yule celebrations too. I've listened patiently, as he regaled me with endless tales of hunting field mice—a mighty catch for his tiny size, and watched from afar as he ploughed the land with his miniature shire horse Chestnut. Even if he's working he'll always stop for a moment or two to share a funny story that he's recently heard.

I annoy him sometimes, just like any younger sister might do. Although I'm a mere two years younger, he will often frown upon what he calls my 'childish ways'; pranking him as I sometimes do by placing a giant heather beetle in his cart as he struggles to pull it along without his knowing.

'Lass, I've no time for your foolery!' he will shout, on catching sight of the heavy, squirming beetle at the back of the cart. 'Some of us have work to do. We don't all live in a Great Tower with servants to do our bidding!'

It will hurt me a little that he doesn't find it funny and rebukes me in the same tone that adults use when they are cross for something or other. It is true also that Jimmy likes nothing more than the comfort of the tiny world of Smailholm, whilst I prefer to wander a little further in search of some adventure or other to ease my boredom. Perhaps even if we were of the same size we'd still have our cross words, those two years in age making more of a difference than our size ever did. Yet I know in my heart that we are the best of friends and always will be.

'But what if Smailholm is discovered?' I ask in a panic, and a little too loudly, for I notice a few of the villagers stop what they are doing and stare up at me, their eyes suddenly opening wider. 'For what a treasure you would be to any normal-sized man—no tiny folk have ever been

7

discovered in these parts and you would surely fetch a heavy weight in gold,' I say, pointedly lowering my voice. I look down and see that some are now continuing on their day's errand, ignoring me. Yet I can't help shivering at the thought of how wide my Uncle Eanraigs' eyes might become if he ever discovered this small sweet place.

'Nay lass, now how is it you are the only giant us small folk have ever seen in all the years of this so-called curse? 'Tis true you haven't put so much as a giant foot wrong,' he says, as he shrugs his shoulders once more and tries to comfort me with a playful smile. I wonder how his confidence in his own small world can be so strong, when he fears so much to step outside it.

'I know, Jimmy, but it is hard for me not to worry. If Uncle Eanraig has his way I won't be around forever. What if I am to leave and there is no one to protect your village? Then there will only be Vargo to watch over you, and you know how *useful* he is,' I say with a giggle.

'Speak of the devil,' Jimmy says suddenly, diving for cover under the roof of the well as Vargo appears by my side. Just in time as well, as giant drops of Vargo slobber splash across the marketplace.

'Where have you been boy?' I say, stroking his golden fur. 'Have you been hunting on the moors without me? Now settle down. Remember we must not get too excited in Smailholm.' I know he is too excited at the smell of the morning's freshly baked bread to heed my words and pushes his wet shiny nose in front of Mrs Jetty's stall.

'Get away with you, silly dog,' bellows the baker's wife. 'Can't you see I'm trying to make a living down 'ere.'

A mass of golden hair led by a red slobbery tongue flops expectantly into the marketplace as Vargo gently lies down and places his black nose right in front of the tiny figure of Mrs Jetty, awaiting his daily treat.

'Oh, be gone with you. Big hairy oaf,' says Mrs Jetty, as she carefully places a tiny piece of bread, no bigger than a thimble to my eyes, into Vargo's giant open mouth and pats his dribbling nose. How she isn't terrified of my golden dog, twenty times bigger than her tiny doll-like frame, with teeth so large and sharp, I really have no idea. Yet every morning—for the last two years since we discovered Smailholm—she has offered up a tiny freshly baked loaf, and Vargo has taken it just as greedily between his giant teeth. In fact, I think, despite all her daily grumbles, Mrs Jetty has a bit of a soft spot for him.

Suddenly, Vargo's ears prick and he lifts his head on high alert. As he stands on all fours and squeezes himself between the tiny wooden and stone buildings, creaking and groaning with the movement, I see Jimmy and Mrs Jetty place their hands upon their ears.

'Vargo *please do not* bark,' I whisper, knowing what is coming next.

'Ruufffff,' his bark so loud in the small confines of Smailholm that everyone in the village covers their ears with their hands. Now the church bell knocks wildly against the bell tower, its unexpected chime signalling Mr Smelt to run outside.

'Be off with you Vargo!' Mr Smelt says, 'and why this fine day do you not have somewhere else to be Wynn?' he says, gesturing his hands back and forth to encourage me to leave.

'Nay, Mr Smelt, my Uncle Eanraig is arriving today. In fact, I do hear his horses now. 'Tis probably what Vargo is barking at. I'm sorry for the disturbance Mr Smelt we'll be gone soon enough.'

Indeed, Mr Smelt does seem momentarily satisfied with my answer, and returns briskly inside the church shaking his head.

Ever since Jimmy and I cheekily placed a giant worm in his church I've always been a little scared of Mr Smelt. What a commotion was caused, a worm after all is no wild boar. I'm sure the children's screams of 'worms, worms, worms!' could be heard all the way back to my home at Smailholm Tower. To little folk big worms can be quite scary I do suppose.

'Jimmy what time is the meeting with Laird Falmouth?' I whisper even more quietly than usual, just in case Mr Smelt should return.

'When the clock strikes seven this eve in the Bull Inn,' Jimmy replies. 'Shall we see you back here lass?'

'I'll try, Jimmy,' I say, not promising. For what this evening holds in this small place or another I dare not think. 'A dance has been planned at the Tower tonight, so I may only be able to sneak away for a few moments.'

Waving to Jimmy, I push myself gently back up from my knees. The brambles scratch once more upon my face, returning my senses to another windy day on the moor. It is such a peculiar place, for I may have been gone an hour or perhaps just a minute. Time in Smailholm is a strange thing. Some days I find myself right back at the beginning of the day that I started hours before. Yet other days, like today, I can see time has been kept in the right order so that the sun, although now in an altogether cloudier sky, is a touch higher and time has passed just as it should have.

Vargo has raced ahead, no doubt on some new adventure in search of food. I look across to the moor to see Smailholm Tower rising above the barren land beneath. With no trees to speak of on this vast murky moor, the rectangular Tower sits atop a crag of rocks known as Lady Hill, where it gives the appearance of resting taller on the landscape than it actually does. This is especially true when viewing its heavy-set and somewhat squat walls from within the small protective barmkin wall that runs around its boundary, and which plays host to our market day, as it always has on the fourth day of each week.

From Smailholm's secret brambled boundary, some distance from my home, I cannot help but stare and marvel at how the Tower manages to stamp the Hoppringle family name so unmistakably on our many acres of land. Yet though just our home it is easily the biggest landmark in the area and can be seen for miles around by passing-folk who happen to glance to the horizon, even as far as Ettrick some 30 miles away—or so they say.

Its four walls, a pristine yellow when it was built by my great grandfather, now bear the dappled grey marks of high winds and rain that have thrashed against the exposed sandstone during fifty unforgiving winters. Climbing to four storeys in all, atop sits an unremarkable roof which slants steeply down to reveal two small ramparted terraces, from where, on a good day, you can glimpse the gently sloping fire mountain of Rubers Law in the distance.

It is true my home perhaps looks a little weary. Where once our lands were rich enough to build a Tower of great standing upon them, over the years the border raiders have snatched away both the fruits of our farm and our cattle. Thrice the Tower has withstood such raids. None in my lifetime thankfully, but how many more it could withstand I do not know. The Hoppringle clan no longer carries the wealth it once did, and I know my father is often vexed with the cost of the Tower's upkeep. Servants and luxuries have long since been kept to a minimum— much to mother's dissatisfaction.

As the sun momentarily blinks from behind a cloud, I see a glint from the small arched-lead windows of the top floor chamber which I share with my two sisters. Just beneath the Tower walls a streak of gold catches my eye. I watch as Vargo weaves his way between crags sprinkled with a dusting of purple and orange heather, racing excitedly to greet the horses that have just arrived at the barmkin gates.

Lifting my long full skirt in my hands, I hesitate a moment not wanting to leave. I already wish I was back in Smailholm with Jimmy. For I know a storm is brewing within the Tower walls.

DEABLIN

Have I not pleased thee of late?

I fear thee grow tired of what I do. 'Tis true the shame grows tall between us—for I am distracted sometimes by finding ways to amuse myself. I have always been a restless soul. But surely you knew that, when you saw my bare toes dangled in the rippling river on the day we first met. Unbefitting a lady you said, but one which made you smile brightly nevertheless.

I do admit my moods have grown so dark over the years. But please, I beg thee sweet husband, do not listen to what they say. I am the same girl you once knew. Down by the river, on a hot summer's day, the cool water slipping through my toes.

I do admit in youth these walls seemed a cage to me, but what view they offer now. Look! As I stand upon the southern terrace of the Tower, I can see her soaring high. Rising free from all around. She catches the wind and lets it carry her weight, hovering graciously before me.

As I peer through the arrow slit, I see her balance a moment in the air; her wings buffeted by the gusts. Then she lifts her great wings upon the wind's force and tilts her head slightly, sweeping down upon her prey.

Oh, sweet Aquila.

CHAPTER TWO

'Anne Hoppringle—why are you not dressed child?' our mother says impatiently as she enters our chamber. All three of us turn around to catch her steely glare, but it is only I who has yet to dress for dinner. My two sisters, Anne and Juju, shoot me pitiful sideways glances, aghast that I would not relish the opportunity to dress for the finest occasion.

An outsider, peering in through the arrow slits of Smailholm Tower, could be forgiven for being confused by the three Hoppringle sisters—alike in name yet so different in appearance. You see, for some unknown reason my parents, Lady Catherine Anne and Laird Thomas Hoppringle, decided to bless us all with the birth name Anne. It is a mercy we didn't have a brother— surely his name would have been Achard, Aldus, Acair? I wonder why they gave such a plain name thrice. Uncle Eanraig says it is a strong courtly name. A name befitting of our family status.

As the middle sister I am known mostly by my second name Wynn, that is until mother's admonishments ring in my ears, her harsh voice echoing up the turret steps.

My eldest sister Anne, some 16 years old now, is said by many to be the prettiest amongst us. Of which she likes to think anyway. I watch her now as she readily twists and swishes the fullness of her dress in front of mother, her dark hair falling in effortless waves to below her tiny waist.

She's been given a new dress by mother and it suits her; laced at the back with cream ribbon, deep plum full bodice and skirt made from the finest brocade. She picks up the hem, the weight of fabric seeming a little heavy, and twirls around.

'You look beautiful Anne, but really people are waiting. Must you all spend so long getting ready,' says mother, not without a knowing smile, for she herself has spent many hours preparing every small detail of the evening ahead. She is wearing a beautiful green silk dress—sent by the Queen Mary's dressmaker no less. The bodice is finely embroidered with golden flowers and it perfectly complements her milky-white complexion and soft auburn curls, pinned so neatly around her ears to reveal the most delicate of necklines.

'Why mother you are always telling me how ladies should make such an effort. Besides I hear that Rubin has now arrived!' Anne says, clasping her hands together in excitement, her cheeks flushing the rosiest of reds.

Rubin is our cousin, Uncle Eanraig's first-born son and I am sure Anne has an eye for him. One day I think they will marry, as cousins sometimes do in the most noble of families.

Mother says that girls of Anne's age should be married by now and that Rubin would make an excellent match. The Hoppringle name must remain strong at all costs, or so Uncle Eanraig says. He says a lot about the family name if you ask me.

'Rubin is waiting for you, so hurry dear child. Uncle Eanraig brings with him such wonderful news,' mother says, then she scampers down the turret steps with an excitement befitting a woman of much younger years.

'I wonder what news that will be my furry friend?' I say as I stroke Vargo.

He has settled sleepily at my feet whilst I struggle to pin up my unruly hair. He looks up at me and then places his head back on his paws, huffing, as if to ask what could cause such fuss.

I quite agree with Vargo, for I have never enjoyed dressing up. I'd rather be exploring the moors. I think mother and father were hoping for a boy, yet here I came. More boyish than many boys I know, yet not able to carry on the family name.

Still my two sisters more than make up for my lack of girlishness. My hands fall to my side, aching from trying to tame the beastly curls that sprout from my head. My hair will never do and mother will be cross. She says I don't make the best of myself, unlike my sisters, who are such perfection in her eyes.

My sandy hair can rarely be tamed by mere pins, and despite my best efforts frizzy curls escape, spilling over my shoulders. As for the rest of me—like my father's, my nose sits rather squat on my face, and my cheeks are a little too chubby I think. The Hoppringles are renowned for their piercing blue eyes, almost turquoise in the dappled summer light, and indeed I do share this family trait with my elder sister and my father. My mother and Juju have brown eyes, so deep and dark many people think they hail from some far-off land. Although it is obvious to those closest to them that this wild land we live upon runs deep within their blood.

I place a hand to my cheek to try and smooth the blotchy red bumps—my skin is coarse from spending too long running against the cutting winds of the moor and nestling in the prickly brambles of Smailholm. I glance over at Anne and watch as she puts the finishing touches to her long dark mane. Delicately brushing her hair behind her ears, she adds a simple pearled comb to one side to keep it from her face. Her hair is her greatest pride and joy and the envy of many, including myself.

My eyes wander downwards to Cleeve, my sister's cat, who sits smugly at Anne's feet. He looks up at me and I'm sure there's a wicked gleam in his eyes as he rises to his paws, stretches that long stretch that only cats can do and creeps his way slowly towards Vargo. There's not a day goes by without some sort of scuffle between the two, with Cleeve always taking great pleasure in tormenting Vargo—much like Anne sometimes torments me. I'm immediately on edge and try to grab the fur of Vargo's neck, knowing it is already too late. For he has spotted Cleeve and the two face each other, just a few steps apart—the battle ready to commence. Vargo, poor thing, often fears his own shadow and faced with Cleeve's sharp claws and malicious hissing never sticks around for long.

And just like that, Vargo is racing to escape across our chamber with Cleeve in hot pursuit; knocking over everything in his path. It is only a small chamber, right at the top of Smailholm Tower and in places you must bend to avoid banging your head on the eaves. There's a small oak door that leads out on to a stone terrace from where you can see across the moor for miles, and this is where Vargo is heading. Before he can get there, he clatters straight into Juju's dressing stool, knocking over her new shawl which promptly falls on Vargo's head. In a frenzy he tries to escape from the delicate, almost transparent cloth, pulling at it so much with his clumsy paws that the material rips clean through.

Silence descends on the chamber and I stare in horror at the scene. Vargo pushes his head through the ripped shawl and sullenly casts his big brown eyes down to his paws.

'Vargooooooo! You foolish beast! Look what you have done,' cries Juju, her shriek piercing my ears.

Anne-June, or Juju as we call her, is twelve and my youngest sister by just one year—and my goodness does she hate Vargo. She doesn't like being outdoors where anything might make her milky-white hands dirty, preferring instead the strings of her harp or her delicate needlework. I rarely see her out on the moors. But this is just as well, for I don't want her following me and discovering Smailholm village. That's my secret alone.

'My shawl is ruined, you horrible dog,' Juju says, swinging her leg back to kick Vargo. He is quick enough to jump forward and clatter down the turret steps just in the nick of time—the shawl still wrapped around his neck gliding delicately behind him.

I breathe a sigh of relief as Cleeve stands triumphantly at the top of the steps then slowly makes his way to curl back at my sister's feet.

'Why do you keep that dog in here?' Juju says. 'Father says he should be outside like all the other animals. He smells so badly and leaves hair everywhere. Animals should be outside!'

'That's not what you say about Cleeve. Why must he always be the exception?' I reply. 'He's always in here, staring at me with those wicked eyes. I really hate that cat and one of these days…' and I pump my fist in Cleeve's face, only for him to nonchalantly close his eyes.

'One of these days what—Anne Hoppringle?' mother says, having reappeared at the entrance to our chamber. No doubt to see what all the noise is about. 'Really Anne-Wynn, this is no way for a lady to behave. And no way to behave towards your sister. Now stop arguing and all of you come down for dinner. Heaven knows, our guests must be wondering where my daughters are hiding.'

Juju and Anne follow my mother down the steps to the Great Hall. Out of the corner of my eye I see Juju turn around and stick her tongue out at me, which makes me even more angry.

She's always so prim and proper when mother and father are watching; my mother's favourite, of course. They are so similar, both with tall and slender frames, long auburn hair and brown eyes. Everyone says Juju will be a great beauty when she's older—just like our mother, who is known throughout the land for catching the eye of many a gentleman. It is no wonder father had such a fight to win her hand.

I look around our chamber, now so quiet and calm. Oh, how nice it would be to stay in the peace of it, or better still, be with Jimmy in Smailholm. But now that the others have gone, I notice the chatter of voices and sounds of merriment drifting up the steps from the Great Hall two floors below. I take a deep breath and exhale slowly, forcing a smile on my face ready to welcome the visitors.

Wary of the evening I may be, but a lady of Smailholm Tower I must be. For this night at least.

DEABLIN

Thee let me dance tonight—and oh how I loved it so. Thee even took my hand and smiled as we danced to the merriest of tunes. I thank thee, my sweet husband.

'Tis a long time since I shared thy company, our children watching over us so gleefully as we glide together across the Great Hall. Yet when I look into your eyes, I see a darkness waiting to greet me. Do you will me to make a mistake, to prove them right? Do thee will it too, my sweet sons?

I am not the mad ole woman you think I am. Not tonight anyway. For I do not fear my mind here and now. The music calms it so. Its sweet tune brings me nothing but happiness, for I am surrounded by memories that grow ever stronger—memories of the young girl who first came to the Tower.

CHAPTER THREE

The Great Hall is noisy, filled with some twenty people drinking and feasting. Tucked in the corner a lone musician plays the harp. He catches my eye for a second as I enter, dejectedly placing his hands back to the strings to play another melancholy tune to which no one appears to be listening. The Great Hall does not lend itself well to large gatherings and I'm not surprised his dainty notes cannot be heard above the din of conversation. In fact, its name is a little deceiving because compared to the hall at Abbotsford, the Great Hall at Smailholm Tower is actually quite small. Square and boxy, it has a fireplace which takes up most of the back wall and only seems to make the room smaller. Six arched-lead windows and two thin arrow slits face out high above the moors, yet because they are all so narrow and let in little light it always feels gloomy inside.

Mother has ensured there's a feast waiting for our guests—a table filled with all manner of pies, fruit and red wine. The smell from the game pie topped with juicy cranberries makes my mouth water with the want of it. Unlike previous years, when many a rainy day has lashed the moors until the ground is boggy and the crops have rotted, this summer has been blessed with more sunny days than most. Our farm at Sandyknowe, further down the glen, has seen a bumper harvest.

Father, mother, and Uncle Eanraig sit at the table, deep in conversation. Uncle Eanraig talks animatedly, flailing his arms about to prove some point or other— until he catches sight of me and sits back casually in his chair, a knowing smile spreading across his rosy red face, already blushed at the cheeks from wine. He nods politely in my direction and I wonder what he is boring mother and father with now. Whenever Uncle Eanraig is smiling there's always some scheme afoot to further the Hoppringle name.

Uncle Eanraig is my father's twin brother, younger by only ten minutes. He occupies the small estate of Nenthomn, some three miles west of Smailholm Tower. Although as children they were very close, time has cast a long shadow between them. Since my grandfather Laird Kester Hoppringle died and passed on the title deeds of Smailholm Tower and warden of Ettrick Forest to my father, Uncle Eanraig has kept his distance. Mother says my father's inheritance has never sat well with Uncle Eanraig who, as his twin, felt the deeds should be shared. Bereft of an inheritance of his own, he has become preoccupied almost to a form of madness with furthering the family name. My father, normally a kind and gentle man, flatly dismisses his brother's musings—and I cannot help but notice the jealousy in my uncle's eyes as he surveys the Great Hall at Smailholm Tower.

'Family, friends, please join with us and gather your drinks,' father says, banging his fist loudly on the table to gain everyone's attention. 'I have a very happy announcement to make.'

As the room falls silent I am suddenly aware Rubin has gently taken Anne's hand in his. He whispers in her ear and they giggle as they walk towards my father at the front of the gathering crowd.

'It is with great pleasure that today I, Thomas Hoppringle, announce the betrothal of my eldest daughter Anne to my nephew Rubin Hoppringle. Please raise a toast to the happy couple. May they share the same happiness in marriage as I have with Catherine, my dearest wife,' he says, and he glances adoringly at my mother.

Loud applause greets my ears and ricochets around the room, its noise further furrowing my already heavy brow. The announcement has startled me, not that I didn't know it would come eventually of course. Yet still, so soon? I wonder why Anne has kept it a secret from me.

Uncle Eanraig leans forward holding aloft his silver goblet. 'I do believe there are yet more celebrations to be announced. Please a toast once more,' he says, as he too rises from his seat. 'Now where are my two beautiful nieces? Please join us as we can also toast to Anne-Wynn and Anne-June's future happiness and success.'

I notice my mother's surprise, a steely glare exchanged with Uncle Eanraig, who smiles sheepishly. A feeling of unease is quickly growing in my belly, winding itself into a fiendish knot. What exactly does this happiness entail?

As I join my father's side he takes my hand in his. His fingers, warm and clammy, tighten around mine and he inhales slowly and closes his eyes.

'What's going on?' Juju whispers in my ear.

'I don't know, but I know something—I don't like it!' I say, my heart pounding in my ears.

Uncle Eanraig glances in my mother's direction and an awkward half-smile plays upon his lips. My mother gives another steely glare in return. Like a scolded child, Uncle Eanraig hesitates, casting his eyes down towards his goblet, as if seeking some solace in the rich red wine. Finally, he clears his throat, and in more conciliatory tone announces, 'Rubin, my dear son, has been appointed to the Queen's guard at Traquair House. Once married Anne and her younger sisters Anne-Wynn and Anne-June are to take up residence at Traquair this winter, where they will begin formal preparation to be ladies in waiting to Queen Mary no less, who will visit on a hunting expedition.' Then he bows his head and steps backwards, as if suddenly wanting to disappear from the crowd's gaze. I watch as he glances apologetically towards my mother, who now looks truly furious.

As I try to take in the words, I feel the blood drain

from my face in an instant. My father's hand tightens even more around mine and I look towards my sisters as they congratulate each other with beaming smiles and kisses to each cheek. Their excitement dances in my direction but as their happy expressions are met with one of horror on my face they look away uncomfortably.

Recovering his composure, his voice almost quivering at his own success, or perhaps mother's impending wrath, Uncle Eanraig says, 'I'm sure you'll agree this is an excellent opportunity for my son and all three ladies and represents the great standing the Hoppringle family now has at Queen Mary's court. So, please join me in a toast to the Hoppringle family.'

Dizziness washes over me and the room turns a mottled shade of grey. Stumbling forward, my whole body shaking, I search with my hands for anything to steady me. My father, sensing my shock, grips his arm tightly around my waist and guides me across the room to the window seat. When the colour in the room returns I look out through the window longingly across the moors and beyond to Smailholm.

'I won't go. You can't make me!' I say, as my stumbling words turn to great heaving sobs.

'Wynn my darling daughter. You have always been the strongest willed of your sisters. Yet despite that wise head upon your shoulders there are some things you must understand. That our family is duty bound to serve the Queen—as any noble family should do,' father says. Yet the sad look I see in his eyes does not escape me and is the only thing to betray his real feelings at losing all three of his daughters at once.

'You cannot make me go to Traquair!' I say, with a rush of anger. I snatch my hand away from his. 'You promised me only when I married would I leave Smailholm. Why would you break such a promise?'

'Wynn. Calm yourself my child. Let that worry fall from your brow. Fear not for nothing is ever as bad as it seems,' he says as he takes my hand in his and gently strokes my palm to soothe me. 'Your mother and I have talked at great length. We could not have predicted such an opportunity for all three of our girls should come so soon. It has been a hard-fought negotiation by your uncle and one we should all be proud of.'

'But father it is too soon. In marriage yes, I understand my place would be with my husband wherever that may be, but now when I am still so young and have so much to learn,' I say, the wetness of tears running down my cheeks with such force I have to wipe them away with my sleeve before they drip from my chin.

'That is precisely why it is such a good opportunity for you to learn with your sisters at the Queen's side as she enjoys her residence at Traquair. You will be back to us in no time for the Easter celebrations,' father says.

Turning to look upon the once merry scene, a sea of blank, questioning faces now stare back at me. Their whispers of confusion fill my ears. They do not understand, how could they? Not one of them is a pawn in the chess game played by the noblest of families in this land—though I have always known that I am to be played at will by those around me for their own gain. Little did I realise it would be so soon.

Snatching my hand away again I stand and straighten my back, tilting my head upwards as if to regain my composure. Of course, I want to turn and say something to them, but the words simply do not want to come. My tongue is dry and sticks to the roof of my mouth. It is all I can do to turn away and bolt for the door, falling against the curved stone walls as I run down the turret steps, barely touching the floor, twisting down and down until I reach the ground floor. Rushing through the dimly lit hall, I push angrily against the main Tower door so that it flies open, banging it hard against the stone wall and shocking me with the noise of my own strength.

The cool evening air wafts over the heat of my hot red cheeks. Tears pool in my eyes so I can barely see beyond. The knot in my stomach grows ever tighter with each breath, until finally I am bent double. The thought of leaving my beloved home—the Tower, Smailholm, the wild moors… How can this be happening?

After a time my breaths calm. There's only one place I want to be right now, so I gather up my skirt in my hands and run, as I have done so many times before, run towards the rocky outcrop on the horizon. Here I will seek solace in another world, so far removed from my own the very thought of it still brings a smile to my tear-stained face. Surely now I must find Jimmy.

DEABLIN

Thee tell me it is for the best, dear husband. How can this be so? 'Tis cruel, you know it.

My home is no longer a place that I can stay, thee say. My darling sons stand silently in the doorway as thee taunt me with these wicked words. I wonder if I can talk to them alone—yet thee never let me. Is Thomas not soon to be the master of this place? Your grey pallor and pained expression give you away. You clutch at your stomach in agony. You think I do not notice? I fear you are soon not for this world, dearest husband.

Why then in your hour of need must thee put guards by my chamber? Do you fear I might slip out the door, without any clothes upon me? Shame, thee said it brought to our family name. You say I danced merry in the Great Hall. Our sons rushing to cover my bare body you say. But dearest husband I cannot remember such shame. What shame do you talk about? I would never shame you, my dearest husband.

CHAPTER FOUR

Where can it be? It must be here. Yet truth be told I cannot now find it! Smailholm cannot be found, there are just too many tears that fall down my cheeks. They stream, one after the other, until they pool at my lips and drip from my chin. I press my face further into the brambles. I've only been unable to find Smailholm once before, when Anne teased me for the shape of my nose, Juju and Rubin looking on. I hated her so much that day.

To find Smailholm I really need to concentrate, and today, like that day, my tears won't stop falling. As soon as I wipe one tear from my cheek another appears in its place. I must concentrate. Please Wynn—think. I need to find Jimmy and tell him that I am going to be taken away from this place. What he might do is surely as small as the world he lives in, I know, but just to hear his comforting words will be enough this eve.

The wind whistles between the rocks, the sun is now low on the horizon and its orange glow does not warm me. I shiver and fold my arms to ease the chill gnawing at my fingers, wishing I'd bought my cloak. I blow on them to keep warm, aware only of how alone I feel.

Taking a deep breath, I peer down once more into the dark space beneath the rocks, where the prickly branches twist and turn. Finally, there it is. I can hear a bell ringing. Smailholm's church announcing the meeting, just as Jimmy had said. I strain my eyes, wishing above all else that I will see Jimmy in the marketplace. As I blink back the last remaining tears from my eyes, there beneath me are the village folk hurriedly making their way into the Bull Inn. It seems everyone in the village has turned out tonight. Jimmy is nowhere to be seen, but I quickly spot his sister Jenny racing across the square with her trusty bow and arrow hung loosely behind her back.

You see, Jenny is hard to miss. Despite the fact she is perhaps the tiniest of all Smailholm folk, she is the girl that catches everyone's eye. I often wonder what would happen if my sister Anne were to look upon her. I think how jealous she would be of such a natural beauty— without doubt equal and more to her own. Jenny's thick waist-length hair, the whitest shade of blond and platted so neatly, more than matches Anne's perfect coiffed mane. For Jenny, whilst no lady does she make, never to place her petite fingers upon harp strings or needlework canvas I am sure, is instead the most daring girl, nay person, I know. Every morning, before the sun has had a chance to creep across the barren moorland, you will find her awaiting the arrival of some unwitting animal. Her tiny figure nestled behind the moss-covered boulders, bow and arrow balanced expertly in the crook of her tiny arm, alert for predators—this day like any other spent slaying the moor creatures that have the misfortune to come too close to Smailholm's brambled boundary. Even though the field mice, birds and occasional rabbit might seem a meagre feast to any normal-sized man, such a mighty fine feast they provide the Smailholm folk in the stark winters when the moors are bare of all else.

Unlike I, whose heart thumps when danger dares to knock upon my door, Jenny will delight at making the most difficult shot, scaling the branches of the highest tree, or squeezing deep down into the darkest cave. Even her dress is unusual for a girl. Her garments are made for hunting on the moors rather than the softer pleasures of a lady, such as music or needlework. A short above knee leather skirt might surprise the eye of many a man if it were not for the tight boy style breeches that sit beneath it that surprise them even more. Across her shoulders a short brown cape made from a heavily woven hemp shields her body from any weather, and the tightly bound leather straps around her wrists provide strength for bow hunting. Her knee length leather boots, adorned with simple fur trim around the calf, provide the only embellishment to her otherwise simply crafted clothes.

Jimmy, her younger brother by one year, often gets annoyed when she challenges him to a race across the moors on their horses. Not because he fears losing, as he so often does, but because it is so dangerous. Without the protection of the rocks and brambles, they are an easy spot on the barren land. Jenny, riding on her much-loved horse Kest, laughing wildly as she teasingly looks behind her, knowing full well Jimmy will slip further and further behind in the race with his more sluggish cart horse, Chestnut.

The stark contrast of the tiny dark horses and distinctive blond riders racing across a solid swathe of green and brown could perhaps be mistaken for the glint of the sun on some unknown shiny object. Or as is true, some other-worldly folk. Yet no one except I believes in such beings, or indeed knows them in fact to be true. It doesn't bear thinking about what would happen if the tiny people of Smailholm were discovered by anyone other than I. Jimmy, who bears the same blood as his sister yet carries both their worries, knows this more than most.

Jenny looks up at me and smiles, shrugging her shoulders as if to say what's all the worry and beckons me so that I might follow. Of course, I'm so big compared to her I cannot follow her far and instead ease myself between two miniature buildings, perfectly cast in yellow-tinged stone by the tiniest of hands, with two tall chimney stacks at either end of the roof. I press my nose and eyes up against the Bull Inn's largest window. Delicately, with just the tip of my finger, I push open the little arch-leaded window to hear the conversation inside.

Unusually, the inn is crammed full of people. The bar is squished tight with pocket-sized folk clamouring for the treasured ale. Flora, the inn keeper, can never supply enough heather and honey brew to keep up with demand, and she shakes her head shouting sternly, 'Be quiet with you, settle down, another barrel is on its way sure enough.'

I welcome the warmth from the small fire, crackling and spitting as the flames lick against the perfectly cut little logs. I catch a glimpse of Jimmy, red cheeked and hot from the heat of the flames, hiding from view in the corner. Even though his face is so small to my eyes I can't help but notice his heavy brow—furrowed into a scowl and heavy with worry at what the meeting may bring.

Presently, a man enters and a hushed silence descends on the rowdy crowd. As my presence at the window has taken most of the light, I can only just make out the man. From his tall, slender gait and flop of the blackest hair, I recognise him to be Laird Falmouth. I too, like the crowd, am a little surprised by his presence—I have seen him so little in the village since I discovered Smailholm. In fact, only once, when I first peered down on this tiny world, has he spoken directly to me, stepping forward to bravely ask my intention when others ran to hide behind closed doors. As he should rightly do as Laird of this small place when the strangest of visitors comes calling. Since then, he has looked up at me from afar with few words, as he does now, with heavy lines of worry on his brow. Now, as always, there seems to be an air of melancholy about him. Deep in thought, someplace else entirely.

He steps forward as if to address the crowd but hesitates, his hand stroking his chin as if in contemplation. He is cladded in leather armour, bound tightly around his small body with straps and heavy lacing on the arms and calves. He clasps his hand around an elaborate hilt fashioned with a silver guard of crosses to obscure and protect his hand in the fiercest of battles. The sword blade itself dangles at his side, the glint of its heavy metal peeping out from an elaborate gilded scabbard— the flames of the fire catch in the gleam of its carefully polished steel. It is unusual to see such an elaborate weapon in a peaceful place such as Smailholm, for aside from Jenny's bow and arrow and the occasional simple hunting spear, there has been little need for such things here. Father always told me that you can tell a lot about a man from the sword he carries. If this were to be true, the elegant weapon certainly places him among the highest lairds of our land, but that it is polished so perfectly suggests perhaps it has been little used in battle.

Finally, he looks up at the crowd, more assuredly this time. Such confidence for one so young—a boyish blush still upon his olive skin. His tall, lithe form has yet to earn the broadness of shoulder and girth of age and marks his 18 years. His black wavy hair, a sleek and shiny crown upon his head, I do decide would almost rival Anne's, and is indeed an unusual marker for a man who carries such a sword.

The Laird releases his hand from the hilt and pushes back the waves of hair that flop over his brow to reveal two piercing green eyes.

'Smailholm folk, I have come here this eve to tell you of surprising news,' he says. 'As many of you know I spend most of my time outside the brambled protection of Smailholm. In the forests of Ettrick and beyond—'

'Aye, we know all about that! You're never bloomin' 'ere,' a voice shouts from the back of the crowd. Some of the villagers stifle a snigger.

At this, Laird Falmouth shakes his head slightly but does not flinch, his expression unreadable, as if he has grown used to these slights.

'Do you hunt, my laird? Whilst you are in Ettrick? I have never ventured so far but I hear the spoils for us small folk in such a vast forest are great. We would all welcome more food to put on our tables at the end of the day,' Jenny says, as she steps forward to greet the Laird with a slight bow of her head, politely recognising his status yet not denying the challenge she has just made to him. She is far braver than I, for I would never dare talk to a man, never mind a laird, so boldly. Yet as always Jenny is bolder and braver than any other in Smailholm.

'Here, here!' a voice booms from the back of the room and an awkward silence descends on the crowd.

'Aye my lady I hunt, as well you might know. For you are a great hunter too—it appears?' he says, a withering smile reaching the corners of his lips as he looks over the bow and arrow strapped to Jenny's shoulder.

'Yes, my laird, many say I am the best hunter in Smailholm,' she says without a blink of an eye.

'That may well be true Jenny, but even if we could fight the giants instead of avoiding their clumsy feet what good is a tiny bow and arrow? This you will find, my lady, is a real weapon,' Laird Falmouth says, grasping his hand tightly around the handle of his sword. 'A slice to the back of the heel with this will bring a giant down in seconds.'

'My bow and arrow are as good a weapon as any sir, as well you might learn, when laced with the finest dark berry poison and aimed directly at a giant's eye,' Jenny says, as she raises her bow in defiance. 'Besides we have found no need for such a weapon here amongst the protection of Smailholm's brambles. The only giant to cross our path is Wynn—most gentle of giants and our friend.'

'I believe you might well have found the chink in my armour my lady, for you are right in your words that here, in the protection of Smailholm, we may feel safe. But out there…' he says, raising a hand, 'well out there it is a great danger that could creep upon us before we have time to act, and that is exactly what I must talk to you all about tonight. For it is not just Wynn, most gentle of giants, that has discovered us,' he says, nodding in my direction at the window. 'It is something far worse.'

DEABLIN

I remember when... When—when is it now?

Ah yes, there it is I can see it now, so clearly. There by the winding stream, on the edge of Ettrick. A hot summer's day. I first saw you.

Thee teased me for my fine silk dress, wet at the hem as I sat on the river bank and dangled my bare feet in the rippling stream—a sign of a noble lady with a spirit of adventure you said. A mysterious nymph hidden in the forest.

As you stopped your hunting party to talk to me, I blushed hot at your words, given so freely from a laird to a young girl, but you smiled brightly and put me much at ease. Like you have done ever since.

You took my hand in marriage long ago and clasped it tightly throughout the years.

You take your hand in mine now, except you do not smile. Your brow wears a heavy frown and I see pain in your eyes. You speak to me but sometimes I'm not sure what you say. How can it be for the best that I am to part from you?

CHAPTER FIVE

L aird Falmouth gulps back his beer and places the leather tankard on the table. With the creamy white froth of honey ale still sitting on his upper lip he addresses the expectant crowd.

'Some of you are young enough, like Jenny here, to know nothing more than our small, safe world that we have peacefully called home. Indeed, only the tales told by my father convinced me our kin once stood tall with normal-sized men. Yet I have always had a strange stirring in my heart that this is somehow not how we are meant to be.

'On his death bed my father urged me to find a cure to our predicament. So, over time I have ventured further and further from Smailholm's brambled boundary in the hope I might find answers. I seek neither to challenge nor scare you, but I do come with news that we must surely act upon.

'Three eves ago I was resting at Ettrick, about to bed down for the night. I was alone once more with only my thoughts, my faithful horse, and the occasional stirring of a forest creature to keep me company—'

'Someone get the harp, for surely it must be time for a gloomy melody.' Mrs Jetty heckles from the back of the inn, merry from her ale. A hushed laugh breaks the silence.

'Shhh,' someone interrupts. I cannot see who has stopped the heckles but I am glad of it, for I am eager to hear the rest of Laird Falmouth's tale, as I see Jenny and Jimmy are too. Laird Falmouth takes another swift gulp of his ale, as if to gain confidence, and continues.

'As the moonlight cast a white glow I suddenly felt a rumbling about my body, the forest floor shaking with the weight of a great arrival. I hid beneath the thick moss, only to peer out when all was silent again. At least six horses were stopped right by me, their muzzles picking at the moss until little was left to offer a hiding place.

'So stunned was I by my sudden predicament all I could think to do was run and hide in the forest undergrowth. But as I ran to the shelter of a fern I was suddenly scooped up in a giant's hand. The giant was just as surprised to discover me as I was to stare eye to eye with him. A border raider I did deduce from his armour, dented at the shoulder plate from some skirmish or other. Indeed, his rotten teeth and a large scar that spanned the length of his cheek suggested a man of low standing who had fought many a battle. The five or so cattle tethered behind his horse suggested hard-fought spoils.'

A barely audible gasp ricochets around the room.

'Border raiders? But they have not raided the Tower for some twenty years,' I say, startled by the revelation. I shiver at the memory of my father's tales of their raids. Two at least that crippled our family's farming stock.

'Aye, my lady. Border raiders without question they were. Unforgiving and most cruel. I've come across them only once before, further north as I watched them raid a hamlet of normal-sized men. Common thieves of no clan allegiance raiding the possessions of every man, woman and child they came across.

'At first perhaps the raider thought he had captured some forest creature or other, but so surprised was he by his unusual prize that he momentarily flinched and dropped me from his hand. Of course, I took the opportunity to escape but not before all hell broke loose and he screamed at his fellow travellers to search about the forest floor for the strange small man he'd cradled in his hand.

'Sadly, it was not I that was soon discovered but my trusty horse who neighed and thrashed about in dispute at being picked up by giant hands. No gentlemen they could have been for they tossed my poor horse between their hands so violently. Laughed heartily they did with every neigh and squeal of pain until finally it collapsed in exhaustion. There they took by the fire to enjoy their stolen mead, but not before putting my poor horse in a chicken's cage. What a sight it was to see the smallest of horses trapped in a cage and strapped to the saddle of a full-sized mare. Both beholden and wary of their vile captors.

'There I sat helpless and sorrowful on the forest floor lamenting my shame at giving not only my horse away but no doubt our small world of Smailholm. For whilst those men sat by the fire drinking in contentment at their new-found prize, they spoke determinedly about finding another just like it. They promised to raid the whole of Ettrick to find more, for they all knew the scale of the prize they had come across and what it would bring to their pockets.'

'You mean to tell us, that you've given us away?' Jimmy steps forward to face Laird Falmouth, fists clenched and cheeks red with anger.

'I bring back this news to warn you all. Whilst I bring with it shame, it is not without hope,' Laird Falmouth says as he takes another sip of his ale, eyeing the crowd nervously over the rim of his tankard.

'And how do you propose we find that hope?' Jimmy says, shaking his head angrily in disbelief. 'For it is you who have put us in such a poor predicament. How can we now ignore our smallness in the world?'

'That is right Jimmy. We must not ignore it at all. Perhaps it has been a blessing of sorts.'

'A blessing?' Jenny says, incredulously.

'Please let me finish my story. For there is more to tell,' Laird Falmouth says holding his hand out to the crowd. There, on his palm, he empties the contents of a leather pouch—the unmistakable shape of four quince seeds.

Gasps and whispers build to a crescendo—for we all know the significance of quince seeds. So rare they are, but rarer still are the folk who farm them.

'That is right. What you see in my hand is quince seeds. Just as I had given up all hope and contemplated foolishly revealing myself to the border raiders in the hope I might protect Smailholm, another hand came down and scooped me up. The darkest, coldest hand that I could ever hope to sit upon. The hand of a moon creature.'

'A moon creature?' Mrs Jetty says, pushing her way to the front of the crowd. 'But they haven't been seen in these lands for years, longer than us small folk have been small. Are we to believe yet more of your far-fetched tales? Has the ale gone to your head?' and laughter piques the crowd's interest once more.

'It is true Mrs Jetty, I expect it is not easy to believe my tales. For I find it hard to believe them myself,' Laird Falmouth says, with a shake of his head. 'As that hand clasped over my body I was taken completely into darkness and the deepest sleep. When I awoke from my slumber the full moon shone. There beside me my horse grazed peacefully, and tethered to its reins was a leather pouch of seeds. I looked around but could see no one. No one at all.'

A shiver shoots down my spine at the thought of those quince seeds cupped so preciously in Laird Falmouth's hand—I know well the tales of their power. Whilst such stories are common place in these lands, the seeds themselves are rarely found. Only from the hands of the moon folk do they grow. For indeed it is such an unusual seed, swallowed whole it is a remedy for the sweating sickness some say, yet when chewed and ground to dust between the teeth it is also said to turn large things small. A trick or true tale I do not know, but even my father, the most sensible of men, once told me a story of his own cousin Bryony, who apparently stumbled across Moon Coppice whilst hunting.

'As hunger rumbled his belly his eyes caught sight of a bright yellow pear-like fruit dangling from a bush. He picked the fruit from its branch and in his greedy hunger gnawed right through to the core, where the seeds caught in his teeth. Of course, no one then, or maybe now, understood the seeds' true power, and so it was he came to chew on their hardened shell and ended up as a miniature version of himself for three whole days. Only when the quince ache left his stomach did he return to his normal size. Yet so afflicted was cousin Bryony by the effects of the seeds' power, he could no longer eat anything at all— he died from starvation some weeks later.'

'But what must be done Laird Falmouth?' I say, shocked at the thought of my beloved Smailholm being found by another of my size. If it were true that border raiders were back in the area I dare not think what they might do to my smallest of friends. The Tower may be capable of defending itself, but Smailholm and my dearest friends, I think not.

'Why my giant friend, isn't it obvious?' Laird Falmouth says. 'Things cannot stay as they are. Who is to say Smailholm won't be discovered tomorrow, or the next day? I for one cannot live in a world where fear lurks with every rustle of wind on the brambles that protect our small world. We have spent far too long thinking we are safe here. Far, far too long. We must find a cure to this wretched curse—before it is too late.'

I see Jenny hesitate before she steps forward,. 'Why, you said yourself Laird Falmouth there are tales from long ago. For we have all heard of the kin that built Smailholm—a cure hidden in the depths of Rubers Law, where the dying take their last breath and where only the true born of Smailholm Tower can release the curse.'

'Jenny I'm not so sure I would believe any of Aunt Agatha's ole tales. You know she was not well when she told those stories,' Jimmy says, shaking his head.

'Why little brother, I believe there be some truth in those stories. We all know Rubers Law has been mined by the quogs for centuries, but very few people have seen inside it, and those who have entered have not returned. Who knows what that fire mountain could hold?'

'Are you suggesting we start at Rubers Law?' Jimmy says.

'I don't know little brother, but surely we need to start somewhere before it's too late and we are finally discovered!' Jenny says, a note of exasperation in her voice.

Laird Falmouth steps between Jimmy and Jenny, holding up his hand to stop their bickering. 'I believe it is true we must do something. In this Jenny you are right. But I don't think we start at Rubers Law. I suggest we start with the moon folk. For surely there is a reason why they saved me from the border raiders and gave me these quince seeds,' he says, looking down at the pouch of seeds he holds in his hand.

The inn falls silent, as if it too is contemplating what to do next, until quite unexpectedly Laird Falmouth looks up at me and asks, 'Are you not true born of Smailholm Tower, my lady?'

'Well, yes my laird,' I stutter, caught off guard by his sudden inquiry. 'I am born to Laird Hoppringle of Smailholm Tower.'

'So, if those tales Jenny speaks of are to be believed then it is you, my lady, of whom we are in most need. A true born of Smailholm Tower to release us from our wretched curse. Rubers Law may be the key, but these seeds,' he says, tossing the pouch up in his hand before catching it again confidently, 'these seeds are a clue from the moon folk. I am sure of it. To be used by us for some purpose or other—to make a giant small perhaps?' he says, a playful smile spreading across his face as the crowd 'ums' and 'ahs' at his revelation. 'Shouldn't we look for the moon folk hidden in the forests of Ettrick? For are they not known to possess the sight? What better gift to use for our cause!' he says, folding his arms and looking up expectantly at me.

It takes me a moment before I realise that the whole of the inn is staring up at me, anticipating only the best of agreements to fall from my lips. My head starts to spin— much as it did earlier in the Tower when a different expectation was put upon me.

'What of the seeds Laird Falmouth? Why would I

have to shrink to travel with you?' I stutter, for I know well exactly what he is implying. Fear unexpectedly grips my throat, tightening it until my words stumble out as nothing more than a whisper.

'My lady you are but a girl, wise maybe for your thirteen years, but still just a girl. How is it that a young girl of such noble birth can travel alone to Ettrick and beyond to Rubers Law without suspicious enquiry falling upon her? Indeed, if she were to be discovered on such a journey would she not be swiftly returned to her rightful place? What better way to ensure the journey's success than to hide her like the smallest of men?'

'He's right Wynn, you would never get beyond the moor without your father's men in pursuit, for you are his most precious daughter,' Jimmy says. 'But, I beg you lass, you must not take this risk for us.'

I gulp. Why has my adventurous spirit suddenly deserted me? Where once I thought it flowed so strong, it has now quite vanished.

I look down at my shaking hands. Where I have longed to escape my frivolous life of needlework and dresses, now I shake at the very thought of any such change. Nothing, not even Traquair, could scare me more.

What if it is Rubers Law to which I am destined? It has long haunted my nightmares. At bedtime my elder sister Anne would terrify me with tales of the ghastly quogs who mine its rock. Of great warriors and noblemen sent by their own families to Rubers Law— the blackest of mountains spitting fire into the sky, beyond the shallow winding valley, beyond Ettrick. A bargain etched in gold between their families and the quogs. A place for all the shamed and unwanted who no longer have a place in the great houses. So strong these warriors and noblemen once were, so many wars they had fought, and now they exist as nothing but shadows, trapped in their beds waiting for a sip of water from ghostly spirits who linger nearby and grow ever clearer in their minds.

My sister's bedtime tales took me deep into the belly of Rubers Law where the blackness is almost complete, with only the occasional flickering of candlelight to give a man comfort. If you listen hard enough you can hear the sound of the blind quogs, tapping against the rock with their pickaxes as they mine the vast stone of Rubers Law for precious gems to feed the insatiable greed for gold of the king quog himself. As and when silence finally arrives, it is time for the great knights and warriors to walk over into the other world. When death eventually comes looking for them a ghostly spirit takes them by the hand and leads them further into darkness, far from sight. Forever. A final warning, Anne whispered in my ear before sleep took hold, that the wicked and shamed always get sent to Rubers Law. Best not be wicked tomorrow, dear sister.

Are my choices too stark to contemplate? A life among the rich and favoured far from my home, or a dangerous quest with my friends? Either way it is clear to me now my life can never be the same.

50

'I can't go with you.' I say, almost shocked that my thoughts have managed to leave my mouth. 'I am being sent away to Traquair with my sisters to train as a lady in waiting to Queen Mary. That's what I came here to tell you Jimmy. I will soon be gone and who knows when I will return,' I say, as tears fill my eyes.

I look down upon Jimmy and Jenny and see them share a look between them—yet nothing more is said. What else is there left to say? For my body and mind is so weary from this night that I rise from my knees and pick up my skirt, aware that in doing so my movement shakes the world of miniature folk beneath me. There's little left to say or do, other than return home, and before I know it I'm back in my chamber, my head buried deep in my pillow and the comforting warmth of Vargo snuggled over my feet.

The only thing I can do is close my eyes to try and stop the tears from flowing until the peace of sleep finally takes me.

DEABLIN

Thee say I leave on the seventh day. I will not my husband. Thee cannot make me. I can hear them whispering now outside my door. What lies they speak of me! Madness? No! Worse—they tarnish me with witchcraft. In times gone by my sight was welcomed, by them and by you most of all. Has it not bought our family wealth when most in need? You forget now I bring only goodness with my gift.

Why can you not see that it is they who cause thy shame, not I? Our cattle stolen once more. Were they blind to it? Or did they have a hand in it? I am not too old to see. How will we survive another winter here?

Do not worry my sweet husband, for I have a surprise to please thee.

Each day my hands grow weaker, curled upon my lap, I do not recognise them from the girl who turned your head so freely. Yet there is room enough for one more deed, for I keep it close, to use one day. Thee will be pleased, I am sure of it. Maybe then, thee will let me stay for a while longer.

CHAPTER SIX

The soft orange glow of dawn creeps through my window. My eyelids are swollen and heavy from crying and I push my feet down under the covers. There at the bottom of my bed, Vargo lies like a dead weight by my feet and I nudge him a little with my toes so that he springs from the bed.

Today I do not want to open my eyes, yet I know at some point I must. I feel Vargo's breath upon my face; his slobbery tongue licking against my cheek. 'Vargo stop that,' I say, eventually opening my eyes. He looks right at me with his big brown eyes, excited for the day to begin. How will I face it when it seems to me that all my world, whether large or small, has changed beyond measure?

I pull myself to sit up on the edge of the bed and look down to see Vargo sniffing at my bedside stool. He laps out his tongue for some tiny crumb or other and then he is gone, no doubt off to find another treat. I think back to last night visiting the miniature world of Smailholm and how I was so cowardly to run away from my friends. How will I ever face them again?

I glance over to the stool where Vargo was sniffing and where the wet of his tongue glistens on the wood. There, a small leather pouch sits in plain sight. Delicately I pick it up, carefully opening it—and empty two tiny quince seeds into the palm of my hand. Who could have placed them in my room—Laird Falmouth, Jenny, Jimmy? Surely, my tiny friends would not have risked such a deed. What bravery it would have taken to climb the turret steps to my room? I wonder, should I now be just as brave? The mere presence of the tiny seeds, barely noticeable to my normal-sized eye, suddenly makes my stomach flip. I look towards my sisters' beds, nervous that they have seen the pouch, but they rest, still sound asleep.

I quietly dress, pull on my thick hooded cloak and carefully tie the leather pouch to the bodice lace of my dress. I creep silently down the steps. Dawn is just breaking over the moor and I know everyone will still be asleep, heavy in the head with mead from last night's festivities. The celebrations must have carried on for many hours, because as I pass the Great Hall the fire is still smouldering in the hearth, the smell of smoke heavy in the air. There by the fireplace a dark figure sits, staring absentmindedly into the dying flames, surprising me by its presence.

'Wynn my dear niece. I didn't notice you there,' Uncle Eanraig says, turning his head towards me as I slink behind the door, annoyed that he has seen me.

'We barely saw you last night. Has something vexed you child?'

Not knowing whether to run or step forward, my anger soon answers my own question.

'Why uncle, I thought you would have understood what vexed me. I am to be sent away from these very walls—am I not?' I say, summoning every ounce of courage, for it is not usual for a lady to question such matters. Yet when so much must change it feels harder and harder to remain silent.

I'm surprised when he laughs, the sound echoing around the empty room.

'Must you laugh uncle?' I ask, annoyed at the cruelness of his rebuke.

'Well my child. It is not a choice we ask of you. It is your duty as lady of Smailholm Tower to do as we require. You are born to such privilege, but that in turn brings with it responsibilities. Besides surely it is no hardship to be amongst the glamour of court,' he says, and with a waft of his hand thinks he has dismissed me.

'I do not want to leave, uncle. My home is here,' I say, my bottom lip quivering.

'You will do as you are told. It is not a lady's place to ask questions, only to do what is needed of them. Besides like your sister Anne, you will soon be of marrying age. I believe Laird Traquair is recently widowed—perhaps such a match would serve to tame your feisty temperament. He may be advancing in years, but that is no matter when the match would bring two good family names together,' he says, a smirk creeping around the corners of his mouth.

As the tears sting my eyes I wonder what I have done to deserve such cruelty. Perhaps he is right—it is just what is expected of me. As Anne has done before and accepted her marriage proposal, maybe I too must do as I am bid. Yet, as I stare into his glassy eyes, eyes devoid of any warmth, I think of my small friends and the warmness of Jimmy's glance in my direction as we joke with one another over some silliness or other. I know right then that I cannot stay and turn and run down the remaining steps without another word.

Outside, the bright morning sun, just peeking over the horizon, warms my face. I turn and gaze upwards, taking in one last look of the Tower, rising high into the sky, its yellow and grey dabbled stone glistening with the dew of early morn. Overhead a mighty golden eagle is circling, its wings buffeting up and down as it catches the wind from across the glen. Whichever way I choose, I know I will surely lose the protection of Smailholm Tower's walls. I look down at the pouch of quince seeds tied securely to my bodice, and in that moment, thinking of Jenny's bravery when mine seems so absent, it seems an easy choice to make. Without hesitation I run towards the secret brambled boundary of Smailholm.

Once at Smailholm's edge I look towards the horizon to check I've not been followed, then kneel in my usual spot at the edge of the brambles. There I carefully take one quince seed from the pouch and place it in my mouth.

As soon as I grind the seed between my teeth a bitter taste seeps over the surface of my tongue and down the back of my throat. It takes a while for anything to happen. So long in fact that I wonder if anything should happen at all. I think about chewing another when my eyes start to blur, as if a white veil has fallen over them. I blink and rub my eyes furiously, terrified that the seed has taken my sight. Gradually, after a moment or two, my eyes re-focus and I gaze around in wonder. For now, I am no longer crouching down by the brambles but instead am surrounded by them, small patches of blue sky just visible through their thorny branches.

I soon discover that it is the strangest thing to be small, my own heart pounding so loud in my ears. Not only has my body shrunk but my clothes too, which is just as well for there was a moment when I was sure I would disappear altogether beneath the heavy cloth of my dress. What magic must moon folk have in their power. I wonder now if they could reverse the curse too?

My stomach aches and I press my hand against it, trying to catch my breath. Breathe Wynn. Breathe. Gathering my wits about me I weave in and out between the brambles, careful not to brush against the sharp thorns that obstruct my path. Eventually, a clearing comes into sight. There just ahead is Smailholm, and the well standing at its centre, its cobbles glistening as the sun peeks through the brambles overhead. I've made it. I rush forward, caught in my own excitement, until all at once I clatter into something, the force of which pushes me backwards onto the ground. Dusting down my dress and cloak, I peer up at the figure who is staring curiously down at me. It takes both of us a while to realise who the other is.

'Wynn? Is that you? How on earth?' says Mr Smelt, staring wide-eyed and mouth agape.

'I can't quite believe it myself,' I say. 'It is a very strange thing indeed to look at you eye to eye after so long,' I say giggling, though of all the people in Smailholm I would not have relished meeting Mr Smelt first.

'Well I'll be damned. Not since my father's tales of normal men shrinking did I know of such a thing,' and with that he shakes his head and disappears into the church. Nothing it would appear stops in Smailholm for long, even when the strangest of things might happen.

Smailholm marketplace is eerily quiet today and I wonder where Jimmy and Jenny might be. Suddenly, I hear a deafening noise of crashing pots and pans.

'Be gone with you!' Mrs Jetty shouts from inside one of the houses. I'm quickly learning that being small in Smailholm is much noisier, and I clasp my hands over my tiny ears to block out the sound. A golden ball of hair emerges from the house and races up to me with Mrs Jetty in hot pursuit. 'Vargo!' It takes me a second to realise that Vargo is no longer a giant slobbering dog whose clumsy paws trample on everything in his path—he's Smailholm size too. Well maybe the clumsy paws still apply, I think.

He jumps up to me, placing his two front paws on my shoulders and licks my face. 'Oh Vargo! I'm so happy to see you. My most furry of friends, how can you be so small?' I say. Despite the fact we've only been apart for a short while, I squeeze my hands around his belly and nestle my face in his golden mane. Pulling out a big ball of Vargo fluff from my mouth, I say, 'Pfft hair everywhere, even when you are now in miniature.'

'Well I'll be damned, two giant creatures turning small in one day,' Mrs Jetty says, who now stands breathlessly at my side, a pot dangling from her hand. 'If only it was so easy to make a small man normal-sized,' she ponders. 'Well child, you were left a little gift last night were you not, and I do believe that Vargo took a liking to those quince seeds just like he does my bread.'

I look in the pouch and see I have only two seeds left, smaller in size now just like me. I remember four in Laird Falmouth's palm. 'Greedy dog!' I say, trying hard to hide my smile. Did Jenny leave a seed out of the pouch and Vargo take it? He has always managed to sniff out the smallest food. No matter I am beyond happy he has. But where are Jimmy and Jenny?

'Where might Jimmy and Jenny be?' I ask.

'They've gone my lady, with Laird Falmouth. They set off for Luds Stoop about an hour past. They are waiting for you, I've no doubt.'

My heart sinks. Why would they give me the quince seeds then leave without me? Now it feels like everyone wishes to send me away. Did they doubt I would come? Maybe so, for I doubted it myself. Before I can start to run Mrs Jetty places a hand over my arm, as if to pull me back from my haste. 'My lady please be careful out there. Where once you stood tall, as it should be for all folk, now you are small. I have not dared set foot outside the brambles and I do believe Laird Falmouth is right to say that beyond Smailholm danger lurks.'

She places a comforting hand on my shoulder and hands me two bread buns from her apron pocket. I have eaten nothing this morn and the bread smells so delicious, but even though my stomach rumbles I know there is no time to wait. I clasp her hands and thank her for the bread and bid a hasty farewell, dashing with Vargo towards Smailholm's boundary.

I run. Faster and faster. Even Vargo can barely keep up. I don't mind admitting I feel so very scared in this new-sized world. In fact, I've never felt so alone, and so small. My heart pounds in my ears and as I weave in and out of the thick brambles, the prickly branches twist all around me, closing in on me like a cage. Finally, I find myself standing out in the open air. The dry ground beneath the brambles suddenly becoming a soft marsh that squelches under my tiny feet. Vargo races ahead and disappears in the tall blades of grass. I twist around and around. Which direction? I've lost all sense of where I am. Where once the moorland seemed so familiar, now the grass creeps higher than my head in places, a vast swathe of green enclosing me. No brambles. No Smailholm. No home.

'Vargo, Vargo!' I shout.

A bird chirps above, the noise getting ever closer, louder and louder. Until I throw myself to the floor and huddle in a ball on the ground. The melodious song now so close, I cover my ears with my hands. Will it eat me? Momentarily, as all falls quiet, I steel myself from fear, squinting open one eye to look upwards. There, hovering above me, in the clear blue sky, is the silhouette of a redstart. Its wings flap gracefully, fanning waves of air in my face and making the curls on my head dance. Presently, the bird lands with a thump, no more than a cat's whisker in front of me and shaking the ground beneath.

Steadying myself, I rise to my feet and stretch out my body so that we stand almost at the same height, staring eye to eye. Its beady black eyes look me up and down warily. Yet, somehow, I no longer feel so afraid.

The flash of deep red across its black tail feathers reminds me of trips to Ettrick with my father in early spring, where flocks of redstarts dance in the air, between the pine scented forest canopy. They are a rare sight on these moors in summer. A travelling bird, heralding a cruel, cold winter if they appear too early in the year. Or so some say. I watch silently as it fluffs and plumps its chest, preening its black feathers with its beak.

Suddenly, a familiar bark sounds in the distance. Vargo. The redstart hears it too, flapping its black feathered wings in protest. Almost immediately, I'm knocked off balance and fall backwards into the boggy ground, my blue dress now caked with mud, great splodges of which I shake from my hands. The redstart launches upwards, cutting the clear blue sky with its nimble black wings. It's then, in the distance, between the blades of grass that dance in the breeze, I catch a glimpse of the white needle-like stone pillar of Luds Stoop. What a relief it is to see something so familiar again. One of countless stone pillars built on the moors to guide travellers from village to village, I have whiled away many an afternoon resting against its cool stone. I jump up, desperate to see it again to anchor my direction. As my eyes peek over the tips of the grass, it's then I see them. There, just beside the white pillar that glints in the sun, I can just make out the silhouettes of four horses and three tiny figures standing next to a golden dog.

DEABLIN

Rubers Law is to be my new home thee say. Thee soothe me with thy words of warmth and stroke my hand knowing that thy touch, so long forgotten, will please me. Care will be taken of me thee say. For my safety and that of our sons you say. Our family gold plundered to take me there.

Be grateful I am supposed to be. Thee promise to visit, yet I know thee won't, for we all know the stories of Rubers Law—those ghastly creatures fill my nightmares as well as yours. Harmless you say they are, but I see a flicker of fear in your eyes. So why, sweet husband, must this be so?

Still, I have one last trick up my sleeve to please thee. Maybe then will thee remember the girl you first met on the river bank.

I hold them close. Three black gems mined from the belly of Rubers Law. So prized they are—to those that hold gifts like mine. They say that the gems mined from

Rubers Law have powers beyond what meagre man can understand. Given as a gift to my mother, passed down to my own hands.

Mother said to use them wisely, and for all these years I've kept them close, tangled in my hair. You will see once more the gifts I can bestow upon you. So, I will use just one—on those blithering fools that speak ill of me. I shall make them leave this place, and thee will be happy.

CHAPTER SEVEN

'What took you so long lass? I thought you'd never get here,' Jimmy says, as I finally reach the stoop. Jimmy offers me his hand, pulling me up a steep bank, upon which sits a thin stone structure. To normal-sized men stoops are no more than a thin stone needle on the landscape, shoulder height, that mark the way for travellers. Most are hollow in nature and with their tiny openings through the thick stone make a perfect place for Smailholm folk to rest. The stoops, dotted from one hill to the next, lead all the way to Rubers Law and beyond. They will serve us well, offering us some protection from moor creatures and the like.

'Well, I thought you'd all left me!' I say, searching for answers in his blue eyes, now so close in size to my own. As I look upon him now I wonder how it can feel so normal when everything else around me feels so peculiar.

'Jenny was sure you would come. I dithered, waiting for you. Hoping. But Laird Falmouth wanted to move ahead to ready the supplies and horses here. Everything is prepared for our journey Wynn. Are you ready?' he says, a warm smile spreading across his face.

Before I can reply Jenny laughs, 'I see you've dressed so well for the occasion,' she says, smiling at the patches of mud on my dress.

I shrug. For I can't help looking at Jimmy. For the first time I am almost the same height as him. Not quite, admittedly he is a hand taller it would seem. I must admit I've never been so happy to see him, and I wrap my arms around his neck and pull him tightly towards me.

'Steady on lass,' he laughs, whilst quickly giving way to the squeeze of my arms. Jimmy and I have never hugged. How could we? Yet I have always wondered how, instead of him sitting on my hand, it would feel to pull him close. It is the strangest feeling to have my arms tight around him and it has sent me quite giddy.

Suddenly I release him, awkward and ill at ease at our new-found intimacy. I bow my head and can feel myself blush and I pray the mud on my cheeks hides the glow. As I speak to him for the first time without lowering my voice to a hushed whisper and look upon his face more closely than ever, I can finally see all the things I'd missed before. The slight dimples on the round of his cheeks, the hint of green in his deep blue eyes and the tiny shape of a dark star on the white of his left eye.

'Was it you who left the seeds?' I ask.

'No, it was Jenny. You think I'd be brave enough to enter Smailholm Tower? My sister is fearless and way better at climbing than me,' he says. I look over to Jenny who winks in my direction and walks off with a satisfied glint in her eye.

'I must admit, Wynn, I am not sure about any of this. Why, a man would be crazy to leave the safety of Smailholm, but just the thought of it coming to harm— well I soon realised that's the biggest fear of all. I knew you'd come because we need to try, don't we? There has to be a reason you alone discovered and watched over us all these years.'

I nod silently and realise that no matter how scared I am, or how far I'll have to travel from home, Jimmy and Jenny are as much my family as any Hoppringle. Besides, now I know I'm supposed to be sent to Traquair and married off to some old Laird, surely this is the better choice? The mere thought of such a marriage sends a shiver down my back. More perhaps than even the thought of the quogs themselves.

I am right to have made my decision to come with my friends—I know I am. If the folk tales are to be believed, that it must be a true born of Smailholm Tower to unlock the curse, then surely it must be I who travels in hope with my dearest friends.

Suddenly, Vargo barks at something or other nearby— perhaps a moor creature stirring. A tiny bark perhaps that might not be heard amongst the chirps of birds, yet one so strange it may alert the moor creatures to our presence.

'That blasted dog! His barking will be the undoing of us!' Laird Falmouth says as he grabs Vargo by the scruff of his neck and drags him to a small opening in the Stoop's wall. I race after them.

'Leave him alone. A dog's bark is how he talks to us. Without him I would never have found my way to here.'

Laird Falmouth sighs, gesturing a small nod of agreement. 'That may be so my lady, but we've a long way to go and many dangers ahead of us. The last thing we need is a dog to be telling our enemies where we are, and enemies there are many.'

Vargo sheepishly disappears into the stoop through the small arched hole cut into the smooth white stone. Following inside, I notice immediately where once the needle-like structure rose to the height of my shoulders, the walls inside now tower above my head. I look upwards, to where a shaft of sunlight pierces through a small hole centred above in the stone. The whitest of clouds in the bluest of skies pass overhead. The perfect chimney I think, as smoke from a newly lit fire drifts upwards and out of the opening.

Beneath my feet, the flat mud floor is dry. I kneel and sink my face into the soft hair of Vargo's fur, watching as Jimmy and Jenny busy themselves, sorting supplies for the journey and readying saddles for the horses.

At the opening to the stoop, Laird Falmouth appears, bending down as he enters. Now I am small, I notice he is easily the tallest of us. With his hand he brushes back his black hair, that flops in loose short waves over his weary brow. His dark leather breeches and wraps are bound tightly around his torso, and I can't help but notice how both my own and Jenny's eyes are drawn to his. It's rare to see such green eyes in Smailholm folk—yet Laird Falmouth's are so green they stand out from the stoop's shadows like the eyes of a cat.

'Let's not argue about this. We have more important things to worry about than a dog,' he says. 'Like how we will get to Ettrick Forest before nightfall. Trust me none of us want to be out on the moor in the dark. Dog or no dog.

'We must be on our way Wynn. I doubt one quince seed will last long, and Vargo has already eaten one of our supply. Ettrick is a three-day ride—once there hopefully soon enough we will find Moon Coppice.'

After a short rest, when the horses are saddled, we leave.

Away from the stoop the heat of the mid-morning sun warms our backs. I look back to see Smailholm Tower, far in the distance. Will I ever see my home again? Goodness knows what mother and father will think when they see my empty bed.

I know I must not look back again, for I fear—as my heart pounds in my ears—I will turn back instead of continuing forwards. And so I turn my head away and mount Strix, my horse for the journey. He is the perfect size for my small frame. Alert and slender-limbed, it doesn't take long to get the balance of him. I stroke his black glossy mane and watch as Jenny gallops ahead on Kest, a flash of white, quickly disappearing through the tall blades of grass. Time to catch up.

DEABLIN

It is done my sweet husband. Did it please thee so?

I crushed one black gem with my very own hands. With glee I watched as they scattered far and wide across the fields, so small they shrunk upon a scattering of the tiniest speck of dust upon their noses. Of course I made sure thee were all away hunting, you and my precious sons, so no harm would come to pass to thy souls. Only to those that voice the darkest thoughts of me.

I did not see where they ran. Yet run they did. Across the vast moor, so tiny their bodies shrunk. 'Tis true the Rubers Law gems have power beyond what man can imagine—and sprites do exist. At least beneath Smailholm Tower.

CHAPTER EIGHT

On the third day of travel we arrive at Ettrick Forest. Dusk is falling. The air grows cold. All around is silence, yet with an expectation that at any moment some forest creature or other will stir.

The trees rise so high above I cannot see where they might end. Their branches dance in the cool breeze, gently swaying back and forth and dusting us with the freshest of scents. Do they feel us walking below, I wonder? Know the hooves of our horses cantering on the parched soil above their roots?

It is said that trees have a sense of even the tiniest of creatures, twisting their roots beneath the ground to reach out to one another when danger is near. It feels almost dream-like to be so small against their giant stature, like an insect caught in the longest blades of grass.

I walk next to Strix with Vargo at my side, our eyes darting across the forest floor where the trees cast their shadows, alert for the slightest sound. We push our way through the clusters of green ferns that carpet the forest floor; the scent so strong in my tiny nose it makes me sneeze.

'Bless you,' Jimmy says, who is walking just behind me with Chestnut, his horse. I turn around and offer a weary smile. It has been a long day with only one stop to eat a small amount of stale bread, our provisions already dwindling on this, the third day of travel. My tummy is rumbling, and after riding for most of the day my whole body aches with the want of bed.

Ahead Laird Falmouth is walking aside his horse. Suddenly he stops. Immediately, I freeze. Silently, he turns and holds aloft his sword, its silver blade rising just above a green fern leaf that is fluttering in the breeze.

We all stop, listening, waiting. The forest is never quiet for long. You might feel like you are alone in this giant place, but now I am so small there seems danger around every tree and under every rock. How terrifying it is to be so tiny. To be so vulnerable to other creatures' whims. I have visited Ettrick twice before, two years past, when my father and his men were inspecting its boundaries. Then, with my sisters, we ran like the wind, ducking between the trees, laughing at finding the best hiding places, knowing that there was very little that could hurt us.

Vargo growls. Ahead, I hear a rustling in the ferns, and sure enough a squirrel appears and stops right in front of us. It is clutching a nut between its rusty red paws and eyes us warily. Laird Falmouth lowers his sword and I feel Jimmy's hand on my shoulder, as if to assure me that all will be well.

'Don't be afraid my lady, animals such as this rarely bother with our kind. Even if they are hungry, they prefer nuts to the slim meat on our bones,' Jimmy says, whispering in my ear so as not to alert the creature. Sure enough, the squirrel seems satisfied that we are no threat and scampers up a nearby tree, quickly climbing out of sight.

I turn to Jimmy. '"My lady"?' I say. 'You have never called me my lady before?' Jimmy shrugs and I see an unexpected flush of red on his cheeks.

'It somehow seems only right now that we are... you know, the same size. It seems more obvious somehow that I am just a farm boy. Your company seems better kept to Laird Falmouth,' he says.

'What nonsense Jimmy,' I say. 'Nothing has changed so far as I am concerned, you are my friend and equal. We will always be so. Besides I think I preferred you calling me lass—like a common wench.' It is a tease, which is quite bold I think—a new Wynn is emerging, one more confident with her place in this new small world. I feel the slightest warmth on my cheeks to match his.

'We will camp in the next stoop for a few hours and then set out to Moon Coppice. I believe it is located on the other side of Ettrick. There is to be a full moon tonight, we must hope for a cloudless sky,' Laird Falmouth says, as he points to a white stone stoop just visible through a break in the trees.

Later as we settle inside the stoop, Jimmy sets about starting a fire from flint and I rest on a fern leaf with

Vargo curled at my feet. Jenny has been out hunting and enters the stoop dragging a snail by its tail, the creature still encased in its shell.

'Yuck is that to eat?' I say as my tummy gurgles.

'We must eat, and it is too hard to kill the bigger animals when you are as small as us. Besides I think you'll find snail stew is quite tasty and will go well with the last of Mrs Jetty's bread buns,' Jenny says.

Vargo grumbles at my feet, as unenthusiastic as I am. I watch as Jenny expertly cuts the snail out of its shell with her knife, chopping its slimy body into pieces and mixing it with a tree mushroom she has foraged. The smell makes me gag and I place my hand over my nose. Undeterred, Jenny places the whole mixture back into the snail's shell and hoists it into the fire like a giant pot, the wood crackling as the flames lick its shell.

'What a strange sight to see,' I say, wondering how I will ever get used to snail stew.

'Wait till you see Rubers Law,' Jenny says.

'Have you been before?' I ask.

'No Wynn, but like everyone I've heard stories of the quogs and their mines.'

'What do you think they mine for? My mother said her jewels came from Rubers Law.'

'Aye, I believe that could be true, Wynn. Precious gems that the quogs exchange for gold provide the finest jewels on the neck of many a lady. But there is one gem they value above all else, or so the folk tales say.'

I sit up, eager for her to continue.

'It is said deep in the rock of Rubers Law lies the bones of their kin, crushed together to create the blackest of all rocks. Held up to the light it sparkles like the stars in the night's sky, and when ground down to dust can be used in the craft of magic by those skilled enough. Some hundred years or so they've been digging their tunnels into the belly of that great mountain,' Jenny says, 'and made their king rich enough.'

Jimmy stokes the fire with a stick and sparks spiral up to the small opening at the top of the stoop. 'They are said to be the strangest of creatures for sure; bat-like in appearance and blind from years living in darkness,' he says.

Laird Falmouth comes up to the snail pot and scoops out a serving of the thick stew with a makeshift bowl made from the bottom of an acorn. He slurps the mixture and smiles. 'This is delicious my lady. A master cook as well as a hunter,' he says, smiling directly at Jenny, and I notice it is a day for blushing—a rosy glow spreads over her cheeks too.

I smile knowingly at Jenny, but I am so tired it turns into a yawn.

'Rest my lady whilst you can. Let's all rest. We have a long journey ahead through the forest,' Laird Falmouth says.

Soon enough my eyelids are closed, the silent darkness taking me. When I wake, it is still dark, and the fire has burnt down to just a few orange embers.

'How long have I been asleep?' I ask Jimmy, who lies next to me, the warmth of his body against mine.

His bright eyes stare back at me in the gloom of the stoop. 'Not long,' he says.

'I do believe you are growing in size Wynn,' Laird Falmouth says unexpectedly, 'Vargo too it seems.' Sure enough, we have. It is suddenly very noticeable when I compare my hands against Jimmy's. They are almost double the size in fact.

'It seems the seed's power does not last long. You and Vargo will need to eat more seeds,' Laird Falmouth says.

I empty the pouch with the two remaining seeds onto the palm of my hand. I eye them suspiciously and look to Laird Falmouth, who nods in encouragement. I fear now the bitter taste and the ache in my belly. Worst still was the way the first seed made my heart thump out of my chest, as if it had skipped a beat and was trying to catch up.

Hesitating, I close my eyes and chew one of the seeds, before holding out another on the palm of my hand for Vargo. 'Better than snail's stew,' I whisper in his ear, not wanting to offend Jenny.

'We must leave now. Your father's men will be out hunting at dawn, no doubt. The whole of Smailholm Tower, and every village thereabouts, must know the laird's daughter is missing by now. Not to mention the border raiders. They would be sure to welcome their reward should you be found.'

'It's pretty dangerous being small!' I say, wondering if it would be better to travel normal-sized after all.

I turn to Jimmy. 'Are you scared?' I ask him tentatively.

'Not of what's out there,' he says, pointing outside the stoop to the darkness beyond, 'just of what danger could befall our tiny world.'

Smailholm Tower—it has been but three nights, but it already feels like an age since I left the safety of my home. I wonder what my sisters might be thinking. They will be angry, I expect, at my disappearance. Anne especially, as the focus will have been taken away from her engagement.

We pack up and ride deeper into the forest. A loud rustle in the tree shakes me from my thoughts. Darkness brings even more unsettling sounds. The wind rustles through the tall pines, their smaller branches now dancing in the light of the full moon. Above is a cloudless night's sky—a vast swathe of black in which I can only just make out the tiny dots of stars so far above. Thankfully, they should help us find our way to the moon folk. Hours go by. Walking silently through the forest. Watching. Listening for forest creatures that might be alerted to our presence.

I pull my cloak tighter around my shoulders, shivering from the chill that has seeped into my bones from the cold night air. Just as I do so, a sudden gust of wind whips the cloth from my grasp. I look around to see my cloak dancing momentarily in the air behind me.

'Wynn get down!' a voice shouts, but before I can heed the command the wind knocks me from my saddle. Suddenly I am high in the air, staring down at my feet which dangle helplessly beneath me. Strix neighing and bucking wildly. Vargo barking furiously. Strangely, the noise of the barks drifts away, getting quieter and quieter as I am pulled higher and higher into the trees.

Squirming frantically, I try to free my arms, trapped by the cloak now wrapped tight around my body. I push and pull my arms with all the strength I have but the tangled cloth is stuck fast around my body. I watch helplessly as the tiny figures below get even smaller until I am so high up in the canopy of pine trees I do not dare to look down anymore.

I close my eyes and feel my body sway. The force so violent that sickness stirs in my tummy and I can feel bile rising in my throat. I'm dizzy and confused and it takes all the courage I have to open my eyes. There, high above the ground, I'm weaving in and out of the tree canopy. I'm being carried along not by a gust of wind, but by an owl whose mighty claws are clasped around its prey.

ME!

Its great claws pinch around my waist and I dare not move for fear it will drop me far to the ground below— for I would surely perish from such a height. We continue to travel at great speed, the owl weaving gracefully between branches while I am tossed back and forth into pine needles that scratch against my face.

With a jolt I'm catapulted against a branch, turning over and over like a spinning wheel as my cloak finally unravels. I land with a thud against the branch of a tree, my arms tumbling free. The owl hovers its wings just above my head and lands in front of me, perching on the same branch and staring at me with the biggest brown eyes I have ever seen.

The weight of the owl makes the thin branch bow and all I can do to stop myself falling is to hold tight to an open pine cone. I stand up, my legs wobbling and my head whirring. The owl and I stare at each other and I notice my tiny reflection in its huge round brown eyes. It blinks slowly.

I stumble backwards but there is nowhere to go. My back is pressed up against the tree trunk. I am trapped! Next to me is a small opening in the bark where two owl chicks squawk. There's no doubt about it—the chicks are hungry and I'm dinner tonight!

My breaths are short and sharp. My chest painfully tight. Gasping for air the panic starts to overwhelm me. Sensing my fear, perhaps, the owl edges slowly towards me, taking its time, pushing me further backwards towards the open mouths of the squawking chicks. Will this really be my end? Eaten by birds? Would it be better to jump from the branch to what would surely be my death far below on the forest floor? I've hardly started on the journey and I'm already in mortal danger. Frantically, I look around for some way to escape. What would Jenny do? She would surely be able to get herself out of this perilous situation with ease. Think Wynn, and quickly.

Pressing my back against the trunk, I spot two sycamore seeds woven into the branches of the chicks' nest. Spinners! My sisters and I used to fly them from the top of Smailholm Tower and watch them spin slowly downwards to the ground. I tug at the seeds and quickly flatten them out until four leaf shape wings sprout from the side of the seed pods. I cling to the storks and lift the seeds above my head.

It's now or never. Do I jump hoping that the seeds will break my fall? Before I can, a flash of light streaks past. The startled owl flaps its wings furiously, wobbling the branch, knocking me off balance.

There's no time to steady myself and before I know it, I'm back in the air and tumbling downwards, spinning around and around in circles without control. I cling tightly to the stalks; willing the seed wings to support me. As I travel at increasing speed everything starts to blur, then suddenly my speed slows and I tug hard on the seed stalks. A gust of wind catches the seeds' translucent brown wings and whooshes me upwards. At first, I twirl in circles even faster. I tug on the stalks to try and slow the spinning, and after a few tries I can almost manage to control my descent. The beating of my heart slows, the dull ache in my chest settling. As I hover in the air, it seems almost peaceful to be above the canopy and look down upon the world below. I watch as the owl flies beneath me through the trees, followed by the bright orange fire of a small lit arrow.

'Jenny!' I cry. Slowly, a numb tingling sensation creeps up my arms, dulling the burning ache which comes from gripping onto the seed stalk so tightly. I'm closer to the forest floor now and through the ferns and blades of grass I see the figures of my friends frantically riding after me.

'Hold on Wynn!' I hear Jimmy shout.

I'm spinning slower now, gliding almost effortlessly between the tree trunks. My frantic breaths calm. How much longer can I hold on? Finally, just when I think I can grip the stalks no longer I glide out from the line of trees into a clear meadow—a carpet of heather illuminated silver by the light of the full moon. It is then I see it. In plain view. Just as the hill crest rises, the glowing outline of a small coppice of twelve tightly knit trees.

My eyes are so drawn to the sight that I hardly notice how close I now am to the ground. The cool white glow of the coppice is so bright. Mesmerising. It could almost be mistaken for sunlight, except that the darkness of the night creeps up against its glowing circular boundary.

As my toes brush against the softness of heather beneath I gaze towards something else that catches my eye—the bright glowing outline of three white-cloaked figures standing between the tree trunks. It is then I realise we've finally reached the moon folk.

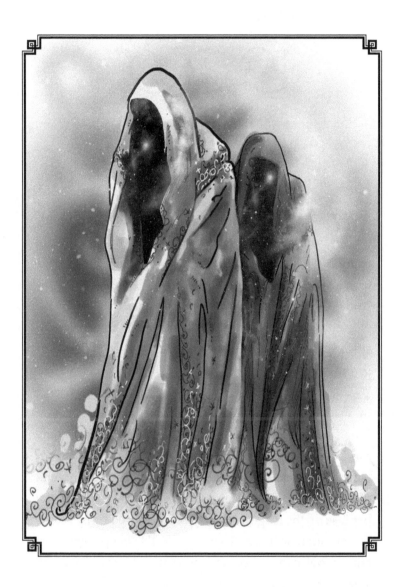

DEABLIN

Why must thee shout at me? The words stumble from my lips as I try to explain my good deed to thee. But I fear it. That look in your eyes. Do I make no sense at all? Thee laugh heartily as thee listen to my stories of sprites. Of my important deed that should have pleased thee. Why did it not, my husband? Even my sons smile, shaking their heads, as if they too have little time for my words.

Thee are angry today. Thee say the fields are barren of working folk—even the blacksmith can no longer be found. A whole village of folk disappeared. How could this be so, thee say as thee toss the words angrily in my face. Then thee say it. The words that I never thought thee could say. That I am somehow to blame, but not because of the magic I conjure but because I bring shame to our family with my strange ways. The people have lost faith in our name, thee say, and that's why they have left. That's why I have to leave.

I stifle a laugh for I know this will only serve to fan the flame that thee set about us. I know what thee are thinking, but do not say. Thee do not think I hear the whispering that I am a witch, a mad witch who must be sent away from our family if it is to thrive once more.

Thee bang the door so fiercely it shakes my weary bones, and there it is closed between us. I know then that I will never see thee again.

CHAPTER NINE

'Wynn are you OK?' a voice mumbles, somewhere above me.

'Where am I?' I say, disorientated. Opening my eyes, I see my friends standing in a circle staring down me. Vargo licks my face.

'You hit your head, Wynn,' Jimmy says, offering his hand and pulling me to my feet.

'I'm well, I think,' I say, but there is blood trickling down my nose, the bitter taste of it tingling on my tongue. With the back of my hand I wipe more blood from my forehead—I feel a large gash on my temple. It is throbbing with pain.

'We must get to the moon folk quickly, it is too dangerous here, exposed on the meadow. They will offer us protection,' Laird Falmouth says.

Jimmy carefully lifts me onto the saddle of my horse. The humming in my head starts to ease. Jimmy rides close next to me, holding out his hand to steady me as I wobble back and forth in the saddle.

The moon, high in the sky, illuminates our path– a perfectly clear night with thousands of stars above. A short distance away, the small coppice of trees is bathed in a strange translucent glow, so strong it hurts my eyes. I use my hands to shade my eyes, as if I were staring directly into the sun.

'You shouldn't have come lass, it is far too dangerous,' Jimmy says. I look over to catch his gaze and see worry etched on his brow.

'I had to Jimmy. For all of you. Besides I don't see anyone else around who is the true born of Smailholm Tower. Do you? So, were you impressed with my flying skills?' I say, smiling.

'Aye lass, expert flying skills—but maybe your landing needs a bit of work.'

I can't help but smile at his jest. I look towards the coppice, the light glowing ever brighter. As we approach the trees, a glowing circle of plants at the base of the trees comes into view.

'Look Jimmy, the light from those plants is strange don't you think?'

'Aye, lass, strange it is. Doesn't it make you feel... a bit... well fearful?'

'No, quite the opposite,' I say, 'I think it looks beautiful,' and I mean it. At the base of the trees sit pod-like leaves, glowing in the darkness. Tiny scraps of pollen, illuminated by the moonlight, dance above the leaves like a snow storm. I cannot take my eyes from the coppice, so spellbound am I by its beauty. Strangely, even though it is a sight like no other, it makes me feel so calm. For the first time since we left Smailholm I feel safe.

In front of the coppice we dismount our horses and wait hesitantly, not knowing whether to step through the glowing plants. Suddenly, a brush against my cloak awakens my senses. So fearful I now am of forest creatures that I flinch. But it is only Vargo, who nuzzles into the folds of my skirt, seeking some comfort. Maybe he is fearful too. Not without reason it seems, because it only takes me a moment to realise that Vargo and I now stand alone in front of the coppice.

Where did the others go?

I look around but I cannot see anyone. They are all gone. Even the horses!

'Jimmy? Where are you?' I whisper. I don't know why I choose to whisper at this moment, when every part of my body is tense with panic. My whispers grow ever louder. And louder.

Eventually I hear their voices. Down amidst the thick cluster of plants beneath my feet. To my surprise Vargo and I are normal size once more.

'Wynn, down here!' Laird Falmouth shouts. 'It appears the quince seeds have worn off. Either that or magic has played a hand.'

'So it seems Laird Falmouth,' I say, kneeling down to look upon their miniature forms—as I have done so many times before. 'But what are we to do now?'

'Maybe they will have the answer. Look!' Jimmy says, and I turn to look towards where he points to see three cloaked figures watching us, their size like mine, heavy hoods obscuring their faces almost entirely. They turn and disappear between the trees, one stretching out a hand, beckoning us to follow.

In the coppice we are surrounded completely by the twelve trees, which have grown tightly together in a perfect circle. At the centre a grassy mound rises on which sits a shallow trough filled with water. There the three cloaked figures kneel. They do not acknowledge our presence. Instead they look down, as if mesmerised by the water in the trough.

Without looking up, in unison they say, 'Come, sit and we will share a story.'

We do as we are bid, strangely without question, and I kneel beside the third of the figures. The water in the trough is as clear and still as glass. There, reflected, is the bright white glow of the full moon.

I look above me to the sky and back down to the water and the reflection is so clear it is almost as if I am looking at the same thing.

My gaze is drawn to the white-cloaked figure kneeling next to me. I cannot tell whether it is a woman or a man, because its body, face and hands are completely obscured with a heavy hood and cloak. Slowly, the creature lifts its hooded head to look at me.

What stares back makes me gasp. Not of shock, nor even fear, but in awe. For the beauty of its features is spellbinding—I do not look upon the face of any normal living creature. In fact, it appears to have no face at all.

Instead, what looks back at me is a limitless blanket of black, punctuated only with the light of the moon and stars. A reflection of the night's sky in all its peace. I look deeper into the folds of its hood to try and observe some face or another—yet really there is nothing at all.

'Don't be afraid child, you will come to no harm here,' the creature says, its calming voice carrying the deep tone of a man. With no mouth or lips to speak of, I cannot presume to know where the words might start or indeed where they might end. They simply dance around my head as if I am swimming under water, the sound of a bird's wings fluttering above the surface.

'It will seem strange at first—hearing us,' he says.

I look over to see my friends peering over the rim of the trough into the water. They do not share in my conversation with this strange creature. Instead, they seem utterly transfixed by the water, their unblinking eyes not leaving the reflection in the trough. I realise then it is I alone to which he is speaking.

'You travel with your friends at great risk. I do believe you hope to find something for their kind—and perhaps for yourself also. Is that not true, Wynn?'

'Sir, may I ask how you know my name?' I say, suddenly realising I have been given no formal introduction.

'Ah we know many such things, see many things, hear many things that you cannot,' he says. 'We have what you call the second sight.' He reaches over to take my hand, and I feel the touch of normal human skin. Yet it is so cold, and black. Black as the night's sky. I flinch, pulling my hand away, but he holds it tight, and instead turns it over so my palm faces upwards. There in the light of the moon, his head bows to examine it.

Only as a seven-year-old had I ever had such a curious encounter. For one day I sneaked down to the kitchen in the Tower. Peeping through the locked key hole of its great oak door, I saw Emma, our cook, sitting with her hands turned upwards and outstretched in the lap of an old woman. The woman, hair as dark as the blackest night and tied messily in a coloured headscarf, her face and ears adorned with the shiniest of gold, studied Emma's palms intently—glancing up occasionally to share some thought or other.

Later, curiosity getting the better of my young mind, I asked my father what I had observed. He told me the old woman was a passing lowland traveller who sold her wares to unsuspecting fools; those who were foolish enough to believe their future could be told from the lines that crossed their palms.

I remember feeling scared, for he seemed angry that this witchcraft, as so he called it, had been brought so brazenly into our home. Later, I found he had stripped poor Emma of a whole week's wages. She never did like me much after that.

'I see you have strength of heart and will,' he says, as he pulls my hands closer to his face of twinkling stars. 'You journey now because you believe in something close to your heart. You must not fear the dread that stirs within, for everything is not quite as it seems.'

I move again to pull my hand away from his, so unnerved am I by the icy touch of its dark form enclosed around my palm. Instead, he tightens his grip around my fingers and says, 'You cannot escape your destiny, child. Your journey has already been written in the stars you see above. I see a great lady with eyes like yours. Deablin was her name.'

'My grandmother?' I ask. The creature nods.

'She was lady of the great Tower. Smailholm Tower. A match made with the most noble laird and warden of Ettrick—Kester Hoppringle. A match made for love as well as gold. Twin boys were born—your father and your uncle. Merry dances were held to celebrate. Yet such happiness did not last.

'Two perfect heirs came at a price. A darkness grew deep inside Deablin's mind. A mind strong in gift, but twisted and strange. She too, like her mother before her, possessed what you call the sight. To see beyond the real world, to places and people that others can't.

'At first she used this gift wisely. Seeking opportunities in the strange things she saw. Her lands grew prosperous and her sons tall and strong. Yet, like the turret steps her mind kept twisting. What once was real became something else entirely. A mistrust grew between the great lady and her people. Her mind crumbled with each whisper that seemed to seep through the Tower walls. Whispers of dark magic by her hands. Was it her fault the border raiders had come?'

'As time passed, Deablin's mind crumbled and her husband and young sons grew wary of her strange ways.

Until one day she took her gift and used it. Unwisely. On the top ramparts of Smailholm Tower she stood and cursed her clan. She cried as she wished them ill but held her hand to her heart and felt the warmth that told her those dearest to her were safe—her sons and husband out hunting that day. For those of her subjects that were unfortunate enough to cross its path that day her magic caught in their noses, making them sneeze, turning them to the smallest of all men. To the brambles they fled for protection, and after a time of reflection they built miniature walls around themselves—the village you know as Smailholm.'

'But what happened to my grandmother, Deablin? For father rarely mentions her name. I believe she died before my birth,' I say.

'His people gone, his reputation sullied, your grandfather believed his wife's mind to be lost. The use of magic carries a heavy price across this kingdom—his lands and title would be stripped away if he should be known to harbour someone with such gifts. So it came to pass that he made a bargain. A bargain with King Atticus—chief quog of Rubers Law. Deablin would be cared for away from Smailholm Tower, and in return he would arrange introductions between King Atticus and other powerful lairds of the land. Deablin is very much still alive, dear child. Yet hidden, like all the other unwanted souls in Rubers Law. Her gift came with a heavy price.'

I have wondered how it could be that my father talked so little of my grandmother. Did he know she was still alive? I have so many questions, but as I open my mouth to ask him, the creature rises to his feet.

'That is all I can tell you my child, I wish you good speed on your journey and gift you more quince seeds so that you may travel safely.'

'But, how can I help my friends? Where do I go from here?' I ask. I fear he might disappear completely.

'Why to Rubers Law, my child, to Rubers Law.'

DEABLIN

Thee take my hand to steady my shaking legs as I climb into the carriage. Thee have eased my heart today with thy gentle words, sweet boy. For I am blessed that thee are my first born, sweet Thomas, so gentle towards me now. Is it a tear I see staining thy cheek as thee bid me farewell? I see none from your father and brother, who took their leave so quickly. I feel sure though that thee will visit soon as promised.

I look up to the Tower where I have spent so many years, the looming darkness of its shadow shrinking back as my carriage rides into the honeyed warmth of the late summer sun. Yet I do not look back as I thought I would. A young girl's soul has emerged from my withered body and I feel excitement bubbling in my stomach as I once did in my youth. A change will be a blessing thee said as thee kissed me on the cheek for our final goodbye. I believe thee, my sweet son.

CHAPTER TEN

As the sun rises, our journey from Moon Coppice begins. The moon folk have given me enough quince seeds to last the journey to Rubers Law. Slipping another seed into my mouth, I chew slowly until the bitter taste fills my mouth. The smaller I get the more my fear seems to grow. There's no doubt the more changes I make in size, the worse I feel. Dismounting my horse, I walk for a while, hoping the rising dizziness in my head will subside. Vargo too is sluggish, panting rapidly with his head hung low.

'Wynn, what troubles you?' Jenny asks, placing her hand on my arm to steady me.

'I feel dizzy,' I reply, 'like last Yule when you drank too much nettle tea only to realise it was Mr Jetty's homebrew. Can you remember how you stumbled and fell over her market stall? Covered in sticky honey you were!'

'Yes, and I've never recovered from that slobbery dog's tongue all over my face,' Jenny says with a pretend punch to Vargo, who looks even sadder and speeds up his pace as if to escape.

'I had to hide from Mrs Jetty for days after that. She never did find out it was me though,' she laughs, but then I notice her shoulders sink and I know something is troubling her.

Despite the jest I am distracted. My thoughts soon return to the night just ended. 'Jenny, what did you see in the water at Moon Coppice?' I ask tentatively not sure I want to know the answer.

'Oh, nothing Wynn, it doesn't matter. Just a trick of the light.'

I know not to push her further. Jenny rarely lets anyone know what she's really thinking. She's always been the warrior among us and she protects Jimmy like any older sister would—except perhaps she is the fiercest of them all. After their mother died giving birth to Jimmy their father took to drink and died some years back, so she's always looked out for him. But as much as she doesn't like to admit it, he protects her with equal measure.

'So, what do you think of Laird Falmouth?' I say, with a smile. We watch as he mounts his horse and kicks hard against its flank to ride ahead.

'Wynn! What do you mean?' she says a slight blush on her cheeks. 'I think he thinks too much of himself. Coming back to Smailholm and expecting us to follow him over hill and glen with some half-baked idea of a better life for us all.'

'Isn't that exactly what we've done?' and blindly too, I think to myself. What might come of this journey is starting to make me feel decidedly uneasy, like the bitter taste of quince seeds at the back of my throat.

'He has no idea how to shoot a bow that's for sure, and as for his sword skills; that blade looks like it's rarely been taken out of its scabbard,' she continues, now in her stride. 'Fie—the Great Warrior! Who doesn't train him to shoot a bow? What use is a sword against the might of a giant when a bow will go straight through the eye? No wonder he drops the Fie for Laird. Fierce Fie Falmouth,' she says, as she picks up her bow and pretends to shoot at his tiny figure, which is currently disappearing over the horizon. With just the tiniest of glints in her eyes, she turns to me and says, 'Besides, you know I prefer blonds, right?' She gives me a gentle nudge then asks, 'Do you prefer blonds Wynn?'

Jimmy is pulling at his horse just in front of us and looks round and rolls his eyes.

'Will you two stop the boy appreciation society? It really is as sickening as snail stew,' he says, his cheeks abruptly turning bright red.

'I think you'll find Laird Falmouth is most definitely a man. Unlike you little brother,' Jenny says, flicking his ear with her bow. Before he can react, she has grabbed Kest's mane and mounted him in one swift jump. 'Better keep a check on Laird Falmouth. I suspect he might need my protection,' she says, galloping across the open moor towards the white needle-like tower of Crest Stoop in the distance.

My cheeks burn hot with the thought of her jest. I know she is teasing me about Jimmy and I stare intently at the back of his white blond hair wondering what it would feel like to touch it. Can you really just be friends with a boy? For a fleeting moment I wonder what it would be like to kiss his rosy lips.

He's always had the nicest smile, all perfect white straight teeth, especially for a farm boy. What would it feel like to kiss a boy for the first time? The only people I have ever kissed on the lips are mother and father. Maybe his lips would feel soft and warm like theirs, but I think it would not be the same, and just as I'm picturing our lips touching I feel my stomach flip quite unexpectedly. It is the strangest feeling, like the quince seeds are dancing and popping in my belly and my cheeks are growing ever hotter.

I think Jimmy senses my discomfort, because he takes my hand in his. His hand is warm and clammy and I notice his cheeks carry the same hot blush as mine.

Since we've become the same size I'm sure something has changed between us. It is hard to say exactly what, but I'm noticing little things about him that I couldn't see before. The tiny dark star on the white of his left eye and the fine creases on his cheeks when he laughs.

He grips my hand a little tighter. 'I'm worried lass. I know I always worry too much,' and he shrugs his shoulders as if to apologise for some flawed piece of his character that irks him. Without reason, I think. 'Last night, when we visited the moon folk, Jenny and I saw something in the water that I can't explain.'

'What did you see?' I ask, eager for him to continue.

'We saw our past,' he says, a hesitation in his voice, 'and our future all rolled into one. I can't really explain it other than it was like a reflection of our lives, like watching it all speeded up. Our birth, our mother dying, our father's grief, his drunkenness, his death, watching us grow at Smailholm, you, our journey here and beyond to Rubers Law.'

I watch as he shakes his head, as if he is trying to order the strange visions. He is uncomfortable sharing these thoughts, I think.

'The darkness of Rubers Law seems so scary Wynn. Just small specks of lights, confusion, that we can't stop where we're going—then nothing. Just darkness. I saw you Wynn, an older version of yourself. You were looking in mirrored glass and combing your hair—in the grandest of houses. You looked so beautiful, yet so sad. The saddest I have ever seen you. You looked right at me and I swear you could see me, for you smiled right back, and then darkness crept in and I couldn't see you anymore.

'When I finally awoke from my trance beside the water and looked into your eyes I knew that this journey wasn't going to end how it should, and I knew you knew it too. The moon folk, I think they gave us a warning. It scared me Wynn. Scared me more than I've ever been scared,' he says, pausing to steady himself.

'When father died and we were left to fend for ourselves I felt so alone and hopeless even though I still had my sister by my side. Last night by the water I felt exactly the same. When I first saw you at Smailholm, this giant girl staring down at me, I was so scared. Yet as soon as you smiled I knew everything would be just right. I just worry because… well I have this feeling like we're walking blindly into something that we cannot possibly understand.'

I squeeze his hand back and feel my stomach flip again. 'I have that feeling too Jimmy, for the moon folk also told me something,' I say, wondering how I'm ever going to put into words what they told me. Yet, somehow, I find the words to tell him about my grandmother Deablin. The magic she used to curse her own clan, and whilst he doesn't question it and I know would never think to place blame, I can't help but feel a little ashamed at my family's place in this tale.

'Jimmy, what if the curse cannot be broken? Will you have to live in fear for the rest of your lives? If I return to Smailholm Tower I will soon be sent away and will no longer be able to protect you.'

'Do not worry lass, as the moon folk told you, our destiny is written in the stars. You cannot escape your fate, only endure it,' he says, squeezing my hand to comfort me.

The sun is shining brightly, yet perhaps sits a little lower in the sky than of late. I think this may be the last of the summer sun before the cutting winds of autumn arrive on the moor. The warmth of the sun on my face and the touch of Jimmy's hand in mine makes me feel safe on this journey of which I know not what the end will be.

We watch as Vargo suddenly breaks into a run ahead of us. He jumps up to try and catch a giant dragonfly, misses and lands head first in a big fluffy golden heap on the grass, defeated.

'That dog sure is stupid, don't you think?' Jimmy laughs. Vargo picks himself up with a disgruntled yelp and immediately starts chasing his tail around and around in circles.

'Maybe,' I reply. 'Though I don't know what I would do without him.' Hesitating I bite my lip for a second before I'm confident enough for the words to pass my lips, 'or you Jimmy, I don't know what I'd do without you.'

We stop and turn to face each other and suddenly silence settles around us; the birds fall silent; the dragonfly has rested its buzzing wings and it is so quiet between us that all I can hear is my heart beating. Jimmy lifts his hand and brushes a loose curl that has fallen over my face and I realise, quite unexpectedly, that my hands are shaking.

Our faces move closer and as I look deep into his blue eyes, so similar in colour to my own, I can feel the heat of his breath—so close it caresses my lips. Instinctively, I close my eyes knowing he is going to kiss me, and I shall return that kiss, my first, with a longing I didn't know I had.

Even though my lips yearn for his gentle touch it does not come. For instead I am suddenly pulled violently by my arms down towards the ground. In an instant my face is pressed so tightly against the earth I can barely lift my head from the watery bog to breathe. I feel the weight of Jimmy's body on top of me and struggle to move.

'Stay down,' he whispers. 'A Merlin! Above us!'

Terrified from my previous unscheduled flying trip with the owl, I freeze. Not that I could move even if I wanted to. Merlins may be one of the smallest birds of prey on these moors, yet they are surely amongst the most agile. Their broad short-pointed wings ensure they can swiftly spring on prey on the open moorland.

Without even looking I can sense the bird is swooping down from a great height to catch its prey—and here I am again. Being small is simply ridiculous. Suddenly I feel its claws skim across my hair, catching my curls and lifting them up for the briefest of seconds. Terrified, I ready myself to be picked up and tossed high in the air. For a girl who grew up in a great Tower I've never liked being up high and the thought of another flight makes me let out a sob.

Beside us a dark shadow appears and I realise it is Laird Falmouth standing over us. He has taken out his sword and is holding it aloft, ready to strike. The glint of light from the carefully sharpened blade momentarily blinds our foe and proves just enough to outsmart the Merlin's incoming advance.

Leaning forward, Laird Falmouth holds the blade high above his head and slashes across the neck of the bird as it swoops towards us. He makes a deep, precise hit, perfectly timed. The stunned Merlin crashes to the ground in front of us, its neck spilling a river of deep red blood until it breathes its last breath and silently closes its eyes.

'That was close!' Jimmy says breathlessly. 'I'm sorry I had to pull you down so suddenly. Did I hurt you lass?'

I turn over to lie on my back and stare up at him, my hand shading the sun from my eyes, and we start to laugh like we've never laughed before. Great big belly laughs in fact. Like having a bird nearly eat you for the second time is the funniest thing ever. I don't know whether it's because I'm so scared, because weirdly I do seem to giggle when I'm most afraid, or if it's the fact that we are both so far from home, my veins full of the thrill of adventure, that is sending me a little peculiar in the head. Either way, I realise I'd rather be in no other place right now. Standing up, I brush what mud I can from my skirt, steady myself and march forward. 'I'm fine,' I say, 'getting used to nearly being eaten now!'

Pointing to my muddy face and bedraggled hair Jimmy laughs and says, 'and you're looking the part again!'

Laird Falmouth steps forward and places his hand on the dead Merlin's head, standing a moment in contemplation as he gently strokes its blue-grey speckled feathers.

'Such magnificent beasts,' he sighs, deep in melancholy. 'It is a shame we are enemies today, how I long to appreciate the bird's beauty without being afraid. But it is better to kill than be killed, and its meat shall provide us with tonight's meal.'

On this journey there seems little time for contemplation, and he sets about quickly butchering the bird. After a while, what meat we can carry is secured in our packs and he urges us to move quickly onwards. 'Come now, we must get to the river bank before we are spotted again. We can wash in the river and we will set up camp for the night. There are too many dangers out here in the open.'

'It wasn't so long ago that I used to train these great beasts with my father,' I say. 'She is a female and would have had young to feed. Still any lady would be grateful for your protection Laird Falmouth,' and with my reassuring words he nods silently and walks ahead, beckoning for us to follow quickly. It strikes me that I know so little about this man who has today saved my life. There is sadness in those greenest of eyes and I think of him travelling alone in search of something other than the small world from which he comes. I hope one day he will find it.

DEABLIN

It is dark here. Like a clouded night's sky, with no moonlight or shaft of starlight to pierce the blackness. For when the candle doesn't flicker beside me the blackness becomes all consuming. The warmth of Rubers Law soon soothes my bones though; not like the Tower where the cold draughts rattle through the walls.

They come to tend to me now and then, grey misty bodies silently appearing nearby. 'Tis true I was frightened at first to see them hovering so close to my bed, yet I have grown accustomed to their presence. They are kind to me, ministering to my needs, a sip of water here and there and whispering tales of my youth. These memories are so precious to me now. I close my eyes wanting to drift into the past once more.

CHAPTER ELEVEN

On reaching Crest Stoop, Jimmy sets about lighting the fire and we huddle around the spitting flames for warmth. The noise from the river outside is almost deafening and I wonder how we will ever cross it.

Just a few days ago that river would have been a tiny brook that I could have paddled my feet in, but now its waves, rippling over the sharp ragged rocks of the river bed, are something to be feared. I look out through the opening of the stoop and my eyes fall upon the black sloping dome of Rubers Law gently rising to a smoking peak far in the distance. I think back to Anne's bedtime tales, which now seem quite meek against its gloomy presence. Even if I were to be at my normal size it would be a terrifyingly large mountain, many times the height of Smailholm Tower, its darkness broken only by the burning fires dotted about its form. Over twenty tall bottle chimneys rise high from its slopes, spewing out thick grey smoke that chokes the air for miles around.

'The quogs have mined Rubers Law for many years,' Jimmy says, as if sharing my unease. 'Those chimneys are great ovens that heat the rock to dust. Hotter than the sun in there, or so they say.'

Even at twilight, it is hard not to miss the fact that there are no trees, grass or plants to speak of about the mountain's great form. Its slopes are pure black, darker even than the night sky. The earth burnt and lifeless where the peak has breathed its flames and scorched the great moorlands for miles around. The starkness against the landscape is accentuated even more by the lush green pine forests, bursting with life, which greet the deathly charred trunks of their ancestors.

'My sisters told me stories of a fire well at its heart that the quogs use to power their mining wheels. Is that true?' I ask.

'I guess we'll find out when we're in the belly of it. Between the heat from the great bottle chimneys and the mountain itself, it sure is going to get mighty hot in there,' Jimmy says.

'Well more than enough reason for a swim before we leave,' Laird Falmouth says, joining our conversation. Without waiting to see if anyone agrees he strips off his cloak and leather wraps down to his waist. I do admit I'm so shocked by his naked chest I can barely look. Of course, just for a moment I do, and it doesn't escape me that Jenny too is staring in shock, her mouth agape, catching flies.

'Not one to be shy are you? There are ladies present. Or have you forgot that?' Jimmy says.

Laird Falmouth steps outside, towards the water's edge, ignoring Jimmy's anger.

My eyes follow his pale white torso as it shines against the heavy dusk air and smoke of Rubers Law. Of course I've never seen a man in just his under breeches before, and I watch as his lithe arms tense as he enters the cold water.

I let out a snigger and Jimmy nudges me right in the ribs and side swipes the dirtiest of looks in my direction. I drop my eyes, sensing a wild streak of jealousy in his gaze that makes my stomach flip.

'Now we've done with the pleasantries, please do call me Fie. Anyone going to join me? It is indeed a fine evening for a swim,' he shouts, beckoning us to join him.

There is no way I'm undressing. Before I can even think to consider such a shame I realise Jenny is hurriedly stripping off her clothes. Daring not to look directly, out of the corner of my eye I can see Jimmy boiling with rage; his cheeks as red as the flames of the fire. Jenny races into the river in just her white undergarments, laughing wildly, her white hair flowing loosely behind her. I notice Fie turns his back, as any true gentleman would, until she is fully submerged in the water.

It is almost dark now and Fie and Jenny are swimming far out where the water crashes its white foam against the rocks. I wonder how Jenny can be so brave. Maybe being small for all these years means you just must be. I do feel like I've been braver since I've been small. Yet maybe not enough, as if I were I'd probably have plucked up the courage to swim rather than sit here in awkward silence with Jimmy.

As I walk down to the river's edge to wash the mud from my face I can just make out their two dark silhouettes in the moonlight's silver shadow, clambering now up onto a rock, half submerged in the flowing river. Jenny laughs at something and I watch as she lies back to stare up at the stars that are shining brightly above us—her figure wet with water gleams in the moonlight.

For a moment I wonder whether to look away. As the water splashes against my face I take a sharp intake of breath from its icy touch. How have they managed to swim so far out in such cold water? But I can't help looking up again and I watch their shapes move closer and Fie slowly leans over to kiss Jenny full on the lips. I watch, mouth agape, as Jenny tries to push him away, but then readily submits and falls into the kiss, grabbing the back of his head to pull him closer.

For the first time I feel a pang of what I can only assume is jealousy prickling my skin and I think back to my near kiss with Jimmy earlier. I look away and walk back to the stoop, aware that I've been intruding on their privacy. There in the firelight of the stoop I can see that Jimmy has likewise turned his back to the river. Later, when Fie and Jenny return shivering to warm by the fire, I see them sharing a private glance and despite the coldness of their skin, a slight blush upon their cheeks.

We eat in silence a meal of roasted Merlin. Better than slimy snails, I guess. The Merlin's delicious flavour makes my mouth water even after I've eaten a whole acorn bowl full. After, Fie announces his plan to cross the river.

'See that hole there?' Fie says, pointing to a large dark hole on the river bank further downstream. 'Well, I suspect there is an otter in there, maybe with young at this time of year.'

'And your plan involves what exactly?' Jimmy says, looking more concerned than I have ever seen him.

'Well, an otter, of course. We are not going to cross this river without some help. We would not last five minutes in the strength of its current further across. I figure otters are particularly good swimmers,' Fie says.

'They also have large teeth. How are we ever going to make an otter take us across a river?' Jimmy says.

'Well if you prefer we could travel at least 30 miles up-river to the nearest crossing? Should take us until... well next month at our current pace...'

Jimmy sits silently shaking his head.

'Look we harness the otter like we would a horse with the reins we have available. We are close enough to Rubers Law to leave the horses and Vargo here now anyway.'

'Whoa kind sir! There's no way I'm leaving Vargo on a river bank all alone,' I say. 'Vargo can swim if he needs to, he's a strong enough swimmer to make it all the way across.'

Fie shakes his head. 'That dog has been nothing but a nuisance and...'

'We are not leaving Vargo,' Jenny interrupts, a furious look on her face.

Fie shrugs his shoulders and sheepishly nods his head, knowing like the rest of us when to fight his battles with Jenny. Before long we have packed up our supplies. Once outside the Stoop, Fie busies himself making a harness big enough for the otter out of two of the horses' reins.

'Here goes!' he says less than confidently. He picks up a burning log from the fire and makes his way towards the otter's den.

'Come Jimmy I will need your help. Jenny and Wynn, you ready yourself at the entrance to grab on. We'll only get one chance, so you better be ready,' Fie says with the authoritative tone of someone who knows what he's doing, and disappears into the entrance to the otter's den.

'The first of many mad Fie ideas I'm beginning to think,' Jenny says, as we all walk reluctantly to the entrance of the dark, foreboding hole.

'Didn't look like such a mad idea when he suggested a swim,' I tease. Seeing her blush again makes me smile; for Jenny rarely has time for blushing, or indeed anything to blush about.

As we wait outside the hole in silence, ready to pounce on whatever may come our way, we suddenly hear the most vicious high-pitched screech. Before there's time to even wonder what's happening a wet bundle of dark brown hair shoots from the cave.

An otter has emerged from the cave furious; its dark eyes gleaming in the moonlight. It thrashes its head from side to side, desperately trying to shake off the makeshift reins which Fie has caught tight around its neck. Fie and Jimmy cling desperately to the reins as it thrashes about. Momentarily it stops and starts to gnaw wildly at the rein. Jenny and I grab tight to its thick wet coat. It's hard to cling on to slippery wet hair, yet I manage to get a grip and hold on with all my might.

Fie kicks his boot hard into the otter's side and we are catapulted forward at great speed. The otter races along the river bank. Around and around in circles we go. Vargo desperately tries to keep up, running behind, whilst the horses whine and kick their back legs furiously in the air, desperate to escape the commotion.

'This is not one of your best ideas Fie!' Jenny shouts, clinging on for dear life. Finally, as Jimmy and Fie pull hard together on the reins the otter steadies and adopts a quieter pace.

'Steady there girl, you are a feisty beast,' Fie commands, as he pulls hard once more on the reins and the otter finally seems to admit defeat. 'No time to lose, we've got her, so hang on.' Fie kicks again into the otter's ribs, this time steering her in the direction of a tree that has fallen and is stuck fast in the river bank, its branches protruding into the water a short way.

At great speed the otter bounces up high and down, gracefully jumping from one branch to another. Without hesitation it jumps from the end of the log and hurtles high in the air. Instinctively, I close my eyes and hold my breath before we are taken into the water in one clean majestic dive.

The coldness of water is so shocking against my skin that I almost lose my grip and gasp for air, only to realise we are deep under water now. The otter glides gracefully between the rocks and thick stems of pond weed, the bubbling current raging above.

Within seconds we come face to face with a large mottled fish, who eyes us suspiciously. Just when I think I can't hold my breath any longer, we resurface and the otter swims gracefully to the side of the river. Gasping for breath, we fall from the otter's back and collapse in a heap on the bank. Fie flicks the reins off the otter and it is free. It shakes its coat, splattering us all with icy drops of water. Baring its teeth in one last show of defiance, it turns its head and swiftly disappears into the darkness.

'Wait! Where's Jimmy?' Jenny shouts rushing helplessly towards the water. I quickly realise that whilst everyone else has made it safely across Jimmy and Vargo are missing.

'Jimmy. Vargo!!' I scream, the hollow sound of my voice bouncing across the waves.

As my eyes adjust to the darkness I see the familiar golden coat paddling frantically across the water.

'Vargo! Here boy, come on boy, keep swimming!' I can see he is struggling against the river's current, and it is then I catch sight of Jimmy swimming beside him, desperately lifting Vargo's head to keep the dog afloat. Before I can even think what to do, Jenny dives straight into the water and swims to them with ease, pulling both to the river bank, where all three collapse.

'I thought I'd lost you both,' I say, rushing to throw my arms around them. 'No such luck,' Jimmy replies breathlessly. 'That truly was the worst experience I have ever had,' he says, looking over at Fie in disgust.

'From where I'm standing, I'd say our trip was pretty successful wouldn't you?'

We all look across the barren moor to the looming darkness of the fire mountain, a little closer now. Uncomfortably so. The dry taste of smoke chokes the air and bright orange embers spit from the top of the bottle-shaped chimneys, darting into the black night's sky until they disappear.

As we clamber our way up the river bank, our steps soon take us from the lush green grass of the moor onto blackened earth, crisp and lifeless to the touch. The final part of our journey into Rubers Law has begun.

DEABLIN

It is time to see the sun once more, they whisper in my ears. They pull at my arms, tug at my nightdress and try to lift me up. It is no use I am too weak and sink back into my bed, shouting for them to leave me alone. Whilst my body has grown tired my mind runs free to a once forgotten place—it is this I seek the most. Why must they pull at me? Why can I not be left alone?

'Tis true I no longer wish to get out of bed. Days, maybe weeks, I have lain here in my own thoughts. Time is a strange thing in Rubers Law. No sun or moon to anchor my direction.

They will not stop today. They push and pull my body until I am upright and carry me forward to a chair much like any other, except that it has two wheels at its base. Like a small carriage they wheel me down the long dark tunnel, lit only dimly with the smallest of candles. I see others, like I, huddled in the cave walls, rocking in their chairs. 'Tis true some are strong in spirit, laughing and shrieking at all hours. Others, once great men of war I think, are so quiet they are never heard—rocking back and forth in their chairs, eyes dead to all around, lost in their own thoughts. Like I.

The brightness blinds me when I emerge from the walls of this place. Finally, when my eyes adjust to the light I observe it is a cloudy day, the sun hidden from my view by the greyest of clouds. Behind me are the great dark slopes of Rubers Law, the air filled with smoke. The dust chokes my throat so that I gasp for breath. Take me back inside thee must, I shout.

CHAPTER TWELVE

Jimmy looks worried, his forehead wrinkling into a frown. 'Is Rubers Law guarded?' he asks whilst tracing his finger along the outline of a scorch-blackened wall, which is topped with ramparts and spirals all the way from the mountain's base to the smoking summit.

'Now, why would anyone want to break into that?' Fie replies, as we all take a minute to study the great smoking mountain. It surely is the strangest, eeriest place I have ever seen. Dotted along the main wall are twenty bottle-shaped chimneys. They rise upwards out of the stone ramparts, each the size of an average dwelling, cast not out of leather or glass but blackened stone. On the side of each chimney there's a small arched door that glows hot with fire.

'The quogs are not known for their hospitality, but they are by nature gentle creatures. Or most of them anyway. Our journey should be safe enough if we keep out of sight of their king. As most quogs are blind and we are small we should not be easily detected,' Fie says.

'And what of the king?' Jimmy asks, still uneasy.

'We would be best to steer well clear—Vargo that means you especially!' Fie says, pointing directly at poor Vargo, who immediately shuffles behind my legs.

'It is true their king has more sight than his subjects. It's said he has used many a healing potion on his eyes. Beside quogs have good hearing and an even better sense of smell. They may be blind, but they are not going to let a smelly, barking dog wander right under their giant noses. They are loyal to their king without question. I mean you would have to be wouldn't you, to mine this place for hundreds of years. The king has a reputation for being particularly cruel to travellers who set foot in his kingdom unannounced. I've heard he's kept travelling tradesman who have had the misfortune to cross him locked in his dungeons for years.'

Jimmy looks more and more sullen with each of Fie's words. 'Well this all sounds like a great idea. Maybe we should just knock on his door and announce our arrival.'

Since our time by the river, I have sensed a troublesome unease growing between Jimmy and Fie.

'We are no ordinary travellers Jimmy. The king would know how valuable we are—the border raiders, remember? We'd be sold off in exchange for a heavy bag of gold in no time,' Fie replies, a sharpness to his voice. 'The chimneys are the easiest way in. Each has two doors at its base. Look,' he says, pointing to a small arched wooden doorway. 'The quogs load the rock into the base of each chimney on a pyre. The heat from the fire burns the rock to nothing more than ashes, until only the precious gems remain. Once the gems are collected they are transported up to the king's chamber right at the summit of the mountain. We should not go anywhere near there.'

'It is a strange thing for you to know all this, is it not?' Jenny asks, curious to know, like the rest of us, how Fie could have such particular knowledge.

'Well, my father was the only laird to be shrunk in the curse. Before, families like mine—families with money, land and privilege—sent any unwanted or shamed soul here. The stories of men and women living amongst the quogs of Rubers Law have been handed down from generation to generation. Maybe it is to scare us I do not know. If you are shamed, you're packed off to live with the quogs—for a price of course,' Fie says. 'Their king knows a good deal when he sees it and such an arrangement has bought him many a bag of gold. But enough of these tales, we must find a way into Rubers Law before dawn,' and he starts to climb up towards the only chimney that is not smoking.

We reach the chimney quickly. Both doors are firmly closed, and no amount of pushing can open them, our tiny bodies no match for the mighty oak.

'Now what?' Jimmy says, slumping to the ground.

'Oh, little brother, must you always give up at the first sign of hardship? Look up there,' Jenny says, pointing to a small opening in the brickwork half way up the height of the door. 'If we can get high enough we can squeeze through.'

'How will we ever get up there?' I ask.

'Climb our way up—silly,' and before we know it Jenny has scaled the blackened stone bricks with ease until she is perched on the ledge of the opening looking down upon us. 'What are you all waiting for?' she laughs.

So, one by one, we start the climb up, with Vargo taking a ride strapped by horses' reins to Fie's back. 'This blasted dog!' he grumbles as he sweats and huffs, Vargo yelping helplessly all the way.

I find climbing hard at first but once I get the hang of it, I'm able to jam my feet into the cracks where the stones meet. I follow Jenny's route and just as I am nearing the opening I catch a glimpse of the ground through my feet and squeal. I don't think I have ever climbed so high.

'Come on Wynn, you are nearly there my friend,' she says calmly, offering me her hand.

Once through the opening, we drop down two small stone steps. The smell of burnt wood hits my nose, tickling the back of my throat and making my eyes water. Heat prickles against my skin.

In almost total darkness, I feel Jimmy grab my hand and we jump down what seems like more steps. Fie lights a twig and we all look around in amazement. What we thought were steps are, in fact, giant clay bowls filled to the brim with strange black stones which shimmer in the flickering flame.

'Ruber's rock,' Fie says, as he looks around the inside of the giant chimney. 'We need to get out of here quickly. We do not want them to start the fires whilst we are in here.'

I look upwards to where heavy dust dances in the air illuminated by the firelight. The top of the chimney is round, larger at its base. After a few minutes' exploration Jenny finds a small opening in the wall. We clamber on top of a pile of wood and peer through.

'I can't see anything!' says Jimmy. Sure enough, there is nothing but darkness, a great sweeping blanket of it with no start or end and certainly no ground to speak of. I blink, searching for the smallest speck of light or comfort. But there is none. Only a vast silent darkness which makes me tremble with fear.

'Let's try something,' Fie says, 'Here goes,' and he tosses a lit twig into the darkness. We all watch to see how far it falls. Curiously it does not. The light does not fall. Instead it appears to float in front of us, dancing up and down in the darkness. Finally, the sparks from the flame dies, far away in the distance.

'Well that didn't work out quite how I expected,' Fie says, with a puzzled expression. Suddenly, though, his attention is caught elsewhere. He places a finger silently to his lips. 'Can you hear that?' he whispers. We listen and sure enough there's a sound of shuffling from behind the second door of the chimney. 'Quogs,' he whispers, 'hide!'

I dart into the gaps between some logs, grabbing Vargo's fur to pull him close, my hand clasped tightly around his jaw for fear he may bark.

We listen in silence as the great door creaks open. The shuffling sound is so close now I almost dare not breathe.

'Clannnnng—' the sound is deafening.

'Clannnnnnnnnng—' something is heaved onto the floor next to us, the logs vibrating.

Vargo starts to growl.

'Shh! Vargo please!' I whisper in his ear.

Silence falls on the chimney once more. Should I dare look? Summoning all my courage I tilt my head upwards, peering through a small gap in the logs. At first, I cannot make out anything in particular, until, quite unexpectedly, I realise there is a creature standing right in front of me.

Something. Is. Staring. Right. Back. At. Me.

I stumble backwards, Vargo wriggling on top of me, desperate to escape my clutch. I cling to him with all my might.

I right myself, grabbing his fur and clamping his jaws shut with my hands again as I peer back through the logs. The creature is still there, stood perfectly still, its face staring silently at me. The horror of it! It is my fault we are to be discovered! I place my hand across my mouth for fear I may scream.

After a time, I realise the creature can't see me at all. For even though its face points in my direction, it surely must be blind—for there is nothing more than thin marks in the shape of a cross in the place where its eyes should be. Of course—it is so obviously a quog. How silly of me. Then again this is not a creature that you can see for the first time and not be shocked. It is a creature so strange to my eyes I am drawn helplessly to stare further. It has a squat wide chin and egg-shaped face capped on either side by two giant pointy ears that stand on end. So large are its ears it is a wonder that the creature can lift its head above its tiny neck at all. Stranger still is its giant bulbous nose and cave-like nostrils that spread almost across its whole face.

The quog starts to sniff at the log pile. It may not be able to see me, but I am now sure it can smell me. Or likely Vargo, who still squirms uncomfortably in my arms. It stops perfectly still, as do I—a battle of wills as to who will move first, until eventually it appears to lose interest and starts its work stacking the round clay bowls.

After a while, I feel brave enough to push my face further into the gap so that I can look upon its curious features once more. The first thing I notice is its huge girth, which is dotted in the middle with a tiny belly button similar in nature to the cross marks found in place of its eyes. It is without clothes except for a simple pair of brown breeches. Around the chimney it wobbles and shuffles, feeling its way with its talons and scooping up handfuls of black rock before tossing them into bowls.

I note it is a hairy creature, wiry thick hair as black as the Ruber's stone itself covering its entire body apart from its huge belly and its nose, which is covered in fine pink fur. With the weight of its enormous ears supported by a tiny neck it wobbles precariously on squat taloned feet and struggles to move with any grace. Rather than walk it seems to prefer to stretch out its long spindly-like arms, which appear as long as its entire body, and grasp on to anything within reach to pull itself along from one place to another. Indeed, it reminds me a little of the small bats that used to huddle at the top of Smailholm Tower and, once night had fallen, scuttle along the great oak beams using their claws.

As it stretches out its twig-like arms it reveals tiny transparent wings hidden under its hairy armpits, I would think too small for any type of flying for a creature of its size. I watch in amazement as it reaches up and grips the inner stone walls of the chimney and instead of setting off in flight scrambles up the brickwork towards the top of the chimney and disappears out of the opening, as quick as even the nimblest of spiders.

'We must get out of here, and quickly,' Fie whispers as he crouches next to me.

'But how?' I mouth back.

'A leap of faith, my lady,' he whispers and points to the opening in the wall that leads to darkness. Any other time I would have questioned this suggestion as madness, but now a waft of smoke starts to drift in front of my nose and I realise that the pyres at the base of the chimney are on fire. The quog must have lit the wood under the clay bowls. No wonder it disappeared so quickly.

As flames start to lick the wood around us there's nothing left to do but to turn on our heels, clamber back up to the opening where we saw the burning twig dance in the darkness and jump into the unknown. Yet again on this most curious of adventures, there's little time to think, and as soon as I reach the opening I close my eyes and jump high off the edge and into the darkness.

DEABLIN

I forget things now. What do you look like? It has been so long in this place I find it hard to remember. Thee have never visited as promised, sweet son.

I wonder how it is possible that I can no longer lift my hand to bring water to my lips, yet I can feel my hands brushing against sweet heather on the moor, the smell of it reminding me of my land beneath the Tower.

Perhaps they come less often now, or perhaps I do not notice, but the ghostly spirits seem quieter. They leave me be—to live in peace amongst my memories.

I am thankful.

I see thy face in my dreams and I know I must wait— for I cannot leave this place without seeing thee one last time.

Will you come sweet son? I beg thee.

One last time may I look upon thy face?

CHAPTER THIRTEEN

'Jimmy!' I cry out. 'Jenny, Vargo, Fie. Where are you?' I reach out my hands to try and feel something, but there is nothing. 'Jimmy please answer!' But no one does, and something strange is happening—I'm floating, being pushed upwards by warm air from below. I feel as light as anything, almost like I'm flying with the bird again.

Gradually my eyes adjust to the darkness. There, all around are hundreds of tiny pin pricks of light, like distant stars in the night's sky. I twist round and round looking up above my head and down between my feet, but there is nothing. Only the blanket of darkness, broken by tiny sparkling lights.

Wiggling my legs, I make great big kicks, just like I'm running. I seem to be moving and after a while I can just make out the cave wall. Two further kicks take me close enough so that I can see openings, the likes of which we've just jumped through. There's no doubt about it,

I am in the belly of Rubers Law, in an enormous cave, neither the bottom nor top of which I can see.

Light after light disappears. I'm floating helplessly upwards. Suddenly, I feel a brush against my back and by swinging my arms to one side I twist my body around as best I can.

'Jenny!' I shout, reaching out to grab her hands.

Putting her finger to her lips she whispers, 'Shhh—'

'What is happening?' I whisper back.

'I've no idea but I do know we're going in the wrong direction. We are floating upwards and not down, right towards the king's chambers!'

We are now spinning face to face. Without being able to stop, our legs pull upwards behind us. Flying like birds—twirling around and around ever faster.

'Look! Over there,' Jenny whispers and sure enough, in the dim light, I can just make out Jimmy's white blond hair a short distance away. Jenny lets go of one hand and uses her free arm to sweep against the air in a giant swooping motion. I do the same with my other free hand. It seems to steady our bodies. We both start to kick our legs in great big frog-like strokes. If anyone were to see us we would surely look ridiculous, yet gradually we move closer to Jimmy, one stroke at a time. When Jimmy finally meets our gaze, he does so with a mischievous smile, his eyes open wide in disbelief and hand on his belly, laughing silently.

Just when I thought it could not get any more absurd, right in front of me, Vargo flies quietly past, helplessly somersaulting over and over. His tongue lolls out the side of his mouth and his legs are splayed in the most uncomfortable position. Could there be a stranger sight than a golden dog floating in the darkness I wonder? I reach forwards to grab his tail, but he floats right past and bangs straight into Jimmy.

'Grab him,' I whisper, but he has already done so and is clutching a big handful of golden hair on the scruff of Vargo's neck. With no control over his legs, Vargo kicks helplessly in all directions, his tail wagging furiously.

By the time we reach Jimmy and Vargo my tummy hurts from the silent laughter. It takes the greatest of strength to hold on to one another and stop ourselves spinning.

Vargo is so happy to see me. He barks before I can grab his jaw to silence him, the sound echoing throughout the cave. My body stiffens in fear, waiting for what might happen next but the cave stays silent.

As we continue to rise higher, a tapping sound, quiet at first, starts to echo louder and louder in the otherwise silent darkness.

'What is that?' I whisper.

The sound moves ever closer and at the same time we keep moving until there is so little distance between us and the rock face that I put my hands out to stop me slamming into it. There, as my hands press against the warm rock, I look beneath and observe the dark outline of a solitary creature. I squint, trying to focus my eyes. There below us is a vast movement, like a wave of black ants moving across the cave walls swiftly and silently. Yet these are no ants. They are quogs! Hundreds, thousands perhaps, climbing up and down the cave walls, tapping at the rock with their small axes.

I watch as quog after quog deftly taps at the rock face, carefully removing pieces that are tossed with ease into sacks strapped to their backs. It is quite something to see how they manage to hang on to the sheer walls with just one thin spindly arm. Their squat bodies are supported entirely by a talon, from which they sway back and forth, mining and collecting the rock with their free arm.

After a while we are brave enough to move again, huddling our bodies in a tight circle with Vargo in the middle. The terror of this empty and dark place so huge in our minds.

'Look over there,' Jenny whispers. Just visible in the faintest of light a short distance away is a horn-like object protruding out of the rock face. It seems peculiarly lavish against such a bleak backdrop, its smooth surface gleaming like that of a gold ring in the darkness. It is similar in shape to the curved horns used to signal the start of battle or some courtly fanfare, I decide. With no way to go down, our path blocked by quogs, we decide to slowly edge towards it. As we clamber inside its shiny rim, a hum of vibrations starts, shaking our bodies from our toes to the tips of our noses. The vibrations are so strong it feels like even the air is shaking. I clench my teeth together to stop them rattling, but it is not enough to keep them from doing so. Slowly we slip backwards inside the horn, a dark void beyond.

'Hold on,' Jimmy shouts, managing to grab onto the rim of the horn whilst we cling to him one by one. Suddenly, Jimmy loses grip of Vargo, who skids and slides on the shiny surface of the horn, his tongue lolling to one side of his face. The vibrations shake his body so much his fur stands on end—one giant spiky fluff ball of golden hair.

'Vargo, hang on,' I shout, but all that we can do is watch helplessly as his claws slip and slide, until eventually he falls flat on his fluffy belly, his legs splayed out beneath him. Gradually, he is dragged backwards into the darkness.

'Vargo,' I scream, instinctively letting go to follow him.

I fall backwards into the darkness, helplessly slipping and sliding, like a smooth pebble tossed across an icy lake. After a few moments I realise I'm floating again. I strain my eyes, desperate to seek out even the tiniest bit of light. Yet alone as darkness shrouds my eyes, all I can hear is the sound of my own breathing.

I tilt my head backwards and flatten out my body, stretching out my legs and arms like a star that twirls in the darkness. For a moment, in the silence, I think of home. Smailholm Tower. Will I ever see it again? It feels so very far away, yet I know there is nothing left to do other than to submit to wherever I'm being taken against my will.

Suddenly hot air rushes beneath me, puffing out my skirt until it lifts up around my ears.

WHOOSH! I'm catapulted out of the darkness into the brightest light, my bottom hitting the ground with a thump. As my eyes adjust to the light, I realise I've landed in what appears to be a giant bowl filled with colourful gems the size of my small hand. Red, green, purple, blue. If these are quog gems, then I must be... oh no... I must be in the quog king's chamber!

Just when I think all might be lost and I start to lose my wits, Jenny and Jimmy fly out of the same opening and land right next to me. I hear Vargo barking noisily yet I cannot see him. Instinctively I shout out, even though I know I must be quiet. 'Vargo!' He duly appears with a loud bark and jumps on my lap, licking my face.

'Well, well, what have we here?' booms a voice from above.

I look up and see two enormous red bulging eyes staring right back at me. The quog king. For it surely can only be a king that takes his place on a giant throne carved from the blackened rock.

He leans over, transfixed with the greatest curiosity, his huge pink-haired belly spilling over his simple linen breeches, heaving up and down in excitement at the sight of us.

DEABLIN

A m I awake or asleep? It is so difficult to tell what is real and what is dream. 'Tis true I open my eyes so little now.

Tip tap, tip tap.

Why must they make such noise? 'Tis wrong, 'tis wrong. Why do thee take my peace? Be quiet thee fools. Except these words that tumble from my lips, my mind no longer seems to make any sense at all.

I can hear him outside my door, shouting at the spirits so they busy themselves, their anger at him in turn bristling in the air. The spirits come, then go, then come. I am alone again.

It bothers me so that I can no longer remember thy face, sweet son. Why do you not visit?

CHAPTER FOURTEEN

'Teeny tiny folk I do behold on this fine day,' the king quog's voice booms, his laughter echoing around the room. I wonder how any such sound should leave his mouth at all, for it is so obscured by his huge nose that is pushed so far in our faces I must take a wary step back. His words snuffle from a tiny hole that sits beneath his nose.

'What a pleasure it is to meet you,' he says.

Unlike the vast darkness of the cave, this room is small and flooded with daylight from a small circular opening above. Overhead, fluffy white clouds move across a deep blue sky. The king quog is right—it is indeed a fine day. The room itself is sparsely decorated but it is most definitely the throne room of a king, for on the floor sunk into the black rock are thousands of tiny coloured gems. Red, white, blue, green, purple—finer even than the jewels of the richest queen. Two large oak doors sit on either side of a central table. Both are closed shut.

I peer over the side of the bowl in which we are trapped and look down to see a large black rock held tightly in the king's talons. Ruber's rock it surely must be; for all the gems mined in this place the one that is most prized is the darkest, blackest stone. What special powers it must possess to be so prized, I wonder? The rest of the fine jewels, that no doubt to anyone else would be prized treasure, are to the king merely floor decorations.

The king, impatient now to view his discoveries, picks up Vargo by his tail with one talon and dangles him in front of his giant nose.

'My, my it is a strange sight to behold, three little people and a teeny tiny dog,' he says, as Vargo yelps in his grasp, his legs dangling helplessly in the air.

'Put him down,' I shout.

'Now my little friends. There is no need to get angry at your king. I am merely pointing out how special you are. There is no reason to fear me when you should know what a great prize you are. It has been many years since I have looked upon folk so small,' he laughs. He turns in the direction of a smaller quog who stands silently by.

'Boy!' he shouts, impatiently. 'Fetch my looking glass.' The boy quog does as he's bid and shuffles over with arms outstretched, blindly fumbling the object into the quog king's claws. The king holds aloft the gold rimmed object and stares through its strange clear glass at Vargo.

The king's eyes are truly a terrifying sight to behold, even more so magnified ten times at least by the glass he holds. Unlike the other quogs, who have nothing more than thin lines where their eyes should be, the king quog has huge bulbous eyes, bulging out unimpeded by eyelids to look in any direction he so chooses. As he pulls the looking glass to one of his eyes, his tiny black pupils grow larger and larger—he is fascinated at the sight of the tiny dog. His eyeballs are scorched with rivers of blood red veins meandering across them.

'Put him down,' Jenny shouts, defiantly pointing her arrow directly at the king quog's face. 'Or I will send an arrow through your eye.'

Still holding Vargo by his tail the king peers down at Jenny through his looking glass. 'Well, well, well, what have we here—another little warrior. It is my lucky day to be in such esteemed company.' Carefully he places Vargo down and puts the tip of his long talon inside Jenny's bow and picks it up by the string. 'Let me take that from you, it looks heavy for such a small lady,' he says, a smile creeping around the corners of his mouth.

Jenny furiously wrestles with him to keep hold of the bow and is pulled higher and higher in the air until she realises the fight for her most prized possession is useless and she can do nothing but drop back down.

'It is a mighty fine weapon you have here little warrior, carved from the finest Ettrick pine is it not?' the king says as he admires the bow up close through his looking glass. He seems astonished that such a small weapon could be so expertly carved. 'It is such a delicate little item, I would be glad to take care of it for you,' and he pops the bow in a small glass jar that sits on a table next to his throne.

'What brings you little folk to my chamber? I am honoured of course. It is many years since your kind have visited these walls. Many, many years,' he says and just for a moment I wonder whether there is a look of sadness in his strange unblinking eyes.

We all look at each other wondering what to say, but stay silent for fear of what our words might bring. Vargo hides behind my legs, burying his nose deep in the folds of my skirt as if it might give him some protection from the thunderous presence of the quog king.

'Silence it is to be then? That is a shame. Maybe later perhaps we may talk for a while.'

I cannot help but notice that he has started to sniff furiously. He takes great big breaths. So great they are that we are almost sucked from the bowl right up his huge nose, and cling together so the weight of our group holds us down.

'Where is Fie?' I whisper. Jimmy simply shrugs. We all look up in horror as the king uses his talons to squeeze his gigantic nostrils together and then sniffs even harder, just as any creature, human or otherwise, might do when trying to blow its nose. As he squeezes tight his two giant nostrils, tiny droplets of water start to trickle from his eyes. Since he has no eye lids to speak of, and thus no way to blink, there is the most peculiar sight of water falling straight from the sides of his bulbous eyeballs like a waterfall. The water runs down his nose before dripping from its tip to soak us.

'Ewwww!' Jenny shouts, patting her face with her sleeve in an attempt to dry it.

'I beg your pardon my little warrior, it is hard to stop the water when it flows,' the king says.

'Are you crying?' I dare to ask.

'Why my little lady, it seems you have much to learn about quogs. Still there will be plenty of time, now that you are here to stay,' he says. As the water continues to shower down upon us and we get more and more soaked, he turns his head and shouts towards the young servant.

'Boy, why are there so few gems today?'

'So, so, soooorrrry, your highness,' the quog stammers, obviously terrified. 'There has been an accident in Low Tairn, a horn is clogged.'

'Well that's not good enough is it! Do you hear me?' the king booms.

'Yeees, yes, your highness. We are looking into it,' he says.

We watch as the king screws a talon into a tight fist and bangs it so hard on the table that it shakes and wobbles the bowl, and us with it.

'Yuuuuuuuuck—' Jimmy says, as he shakes his arms, droplets of water falling from his fingertips. 'I didn't think you could get any worse than Vargo slobber.' Were we not in such a precarious position I would laugh.

We watch as the king reaches into a small leather pouch tied around his neck. He takes out a pinch of a dust-like substance, places it under his nose and sniffs.

'Ah, that's better,' he says, and almost immediately the water stops running from his eyes. 'Now I can see again. It is but a sad way to live—beholden to these blasted potions.'

He scoops us up one by one and delicately, like some treasured gems, places us in the glass jar with Jenny's bow. 'I have business to attend to. You will be safe here until I return,' and with these words he and the boy quog shuffle out of the great oak door, which creaks then bangs as it shuts behind them.

DEABLIN

Ech day me comëth tydinges thre,
For wel swithë sore ben he:
The on is that Ich shal hennë,
That other that Ich not whennë,
The thriddë is my mestë carë,
That Ich not whider Ich shal far.

(Every day I am plagued by three thoughts—
A heavy weight on my soul.
First, that my time is finite
Second, I know not when I will depart
But it is the third that torments me most
That there is no way to know where I'll go.)

CHAPTER FIFTEEN

After a while, when silence has fallen once more upon our ears, one by one we become brave enough to speak.

'That was disgusting. Did you see how much water came from his eyes?' Jimmy says, as he wipes the remaining dampness from his brow.

'Sometimes little brother you really do surprise me. Don't you think we've more important things to complain about?' Jenny says decisively. 'Like getting out of here and find Fie.'

'Well he's been some use, hasn't he? Whilst we've been up here entertaining the king he's nowhere to be seen,' Jimmy replies, grumpily sliding his back down the glass and slumping at our feet.

'Why must you always mope about everything, little brother? Nothing good will come of sitting here feeling sorry for ourselves.'

'We need to stop arguing and think of a way out,' I interrupt. 'The king is sure to be back soon.'

'What do you suggest then Jenny?' Jimmy replies with a scowl.

Jenny walks around the base of the jar, one, two, three laps, around and around, as if willing a magical door to open. Even when I place my nose against the glass and peer right out it is impossible to see much except shadows in the room beyond. We are trapped in a cage, like Fie's horse, I think. He was right—all creatures, even those as peculiar as quogs, will delight in keeping us captive. To dance and sing and keep them merry, until we satisfy their curiosity and they grow tired of us and leave us in a jar to die of thirst. The bitter taste of fear rises in my throat, squeezing the air from my lungs.

'We must get out of here. I can't breathe,' I say, choking back sobs.

'It will be alright lass,' and I feel the familiar warmth of Jimmy who stands beside me, his arms wrapped around my shoulders. 'Jenny will work out a way,' he says softly.

'Why, little brother, must it always be I that has to get us out of such messes? Are you not a man yourself?' Jenny says, fixing a withering glare in his direction.

'Why there is no doubt that I carry myself more like a man than you do a lady. I saw you Jenny, with Fie, kissing in just your undergarments, brazen as a common hussy in full view of everyone,' he says, arms folded angrily.

'And what of it—little brother? You'll be best placed not to question it whilst we are trapped together in such a small place,' she says, her teeth clamped tight in anger.

It is all I can do to stand between them to stop them fighting. I've seen them fight each other only once before, when Jimmy saw Jenny kissing Tom Jetty. It was only Mrs Jetty who stopped Jenny giving her little brother a black eye that day.

'Stop it!' I cry, tears trickling from my eyes. 'We have to stop arguing and get out of here, before it's too late.'

When silence finally descends, we look around helplessly for ways to escape.

Vargo barks. His tail wagging furiously. I bend down. 'What is it boy?' I ask, 'Is that nasty creature returning?'

'No, I don't think so, but look there's someone standing there. Look,' Jimmy says, pointing to the small dark figure on the other side of the jar.

'Fie. Is that you?' Jenny shouts, pressing her nose up against the glass.

'How on earth did you get into there?' Fie shouts back.

'No time to explain, we need to get out of here,' Jenny shouts.

Suddenly Jimmy stands up, 'I have an idea. Of course, it may not work but—'

'Yes, yes, little brother, we need to hurry—quicker!'

'Well, let's try and rock the jar from side to side. Maybe if we sit on each other's shoulders and push against the jar, and Fie pushes from the outside, it will be enough so that we can tip it over,' he says.

'Fie, can you push from your side as hard as you can?' Jenny shouts.

'I'll give it a go!' Fie shouts.

We run to the opposite side of the jar to Fie and Jenny climbs to sit on Jimmy's shoulders 'Push. Now,' Jenny shouts. We all push and push. Gradually the jar starts to tip.

'Push harder,' Jimmy shouts and I wince at the ache in my arms from pushing at the glass. Suddenly the jar starts to rock from side to side, until it balances precariously on one edge, before tipping over.

CRASH!

The jar falls on its side, still intact. Right before us stands Fie.

'What kept you so long?' Fie smiles, locking eyes with Jenny.

'Fie!' Jenny says as she runs out of the jar towards him, Vargo following excitedly. Jimmy grabs my hand and tries to steady us both, but it's too late. The jar is rocking back and forth on its side and Jenny and Vargo's run has caused it to start rolling right towards the edge of the table.

'Run. Now!' Jimmy shouts, tugging my arm until we are jumping from the jar to land in a crumpled heap on the table. I watch, mouth open, as the jar rolls off the table and smashes onto the floor beneath, a thousand pieces of glass scattered in all directions. We peer over the edge of the table and then at each other and realise what a lucky escape we've all had.

'Well that's just alerted the whole of Rubers Law.' Jenny curses.

'Shh,' Fie whispers, raising a finger to his lips. Through the silence we can hear the now familiar shuffling sound of quogs getting closer and closer to the door of the king's chamber.

'It appears the quogs are no longer distracted,' Fie says.

'Distracted by what?' Jimmy asks.

'Well I may have blocked one of their horns on the way up here. A little distraction shall we say, whilst I looked for you.' There's a satisfied smile upon his face.

'I'd say well done, except I'm not sure how we'll get down from this table,' Jenny says.

'Why, the same way I came up,' Fie says, and we watch as he runs to one corner of the table and pulls on a rope that he's attached to the top of the table's leg.

'But what about Vargo?' I say.

'That blasted dog,' Fie grumbles. 'He'll just have to come for a ride on my back again I suppose.' And so, one by one, with Vargo tied to Fie's back, we all climb down the rope.

'Where now?' Jimmy says, looking around the room for some means to escape.

'Over there,' Jenny says, diving towards one of the great oak doors. The base of the door has just enough of a gap for us all to squeeze under and we find ourselves in another room, similar in size but empty except for strange green vines, that seem to cling to each corner of the room. On the cave wall is a series of marks that have been carved into the black rock face. Strange birds, numerous wheels, a river and a large waterfall are all expertly carved into the rock by hand, like drawings on parchment. Underneath the carving of the river sit small cave-like holes. As I trace my fingers across the carvings, in awe of how beautiful it is, I suddenly realise what I'm looking at.

'Wait. I know what this is. It's a carving of Rubers Law. Of the kingdom. It's carved into the rock because of the king's poor sight. He doesn't read it with his eyes, but by touch,' I say excitedly. 'Father showed me a similar drawing in a cave in Ettrick Forest.'

'Maybe we can use it to our advantage,' Fie says.

'You may well be right. Look we are here—this must indicate the king's chamber,' I say pointing to a throne. At its feet is the imprint of six coloured sparkling gems. I continue to trace my finger sideways to where there is a small tunnel carved into the rock. It leads to a wheel and then downwards through wave-like swirls.

'Water. The wheel is a waterwheel, powering the mine. Look how the swirls hit the base of Rubers Law—the fire mountain's heart.' Carved on the map below the water is a large pool from which giant clouds balloon up.

'These are the caves,' I say excitedly pointing to tunnels at the bottom of the map. 'Surely that is where Deablin must be. It has to be.'

'Look,' Fie says pointing to the waterwheel. 'We'll use the water to get us down. In the heart of Rubers Law, where the air is hot our tiny bodies would just rise higher, but the force of the water should take us downwards.'

Suddenly we hear an almighty howl all about us.

'RAAAA—!'

The shout is so loud, and it is coming from behind the door to the throne room.

Jenny gulps, 'Time to leave. The king seems to have discovered his prized little folk have disappeared.'

'Now where?' Fie says. We all look around the room which is completely empty of anywhere to hide. We watch as Jimmy runs towards green vines that grow up the wall in its far corner.

'Perhaps we can hide behind these?' he says, disappearing completely. After a moment he reappears. 'I think I've found a way out,' he says. 'There seems to be some sort of gap in the rock face. A tunnel of sorts.'

Behind me I can hear the grind of metal on metal as the latch to the throne room door tilts upwards. I don't stop to think and run as fast as I can to Jimmy. I scramble through the opening and follow him into the darkness.

DEABLIN

'Tis cruel, 'tis cruel, the god who looks down upon me. Come quick thee blithering fool for I am sick of waiting! Why must thee taunt me with these spirits so! They pull at my gown, and wickedly bruise me with their coarse hands. So cruel they are.

No one cares about me, I am sure. Locked away in this dark place all these years. I am paying dearly now for my past sins—'tis true. They will not break me though, for thee will come soon—sure enough, I know it.

Enough now, don't sard with me thee fool, come why don't thee?

By God's bones I demand it.

CHAPTER SIXTEEN

The tunnel is so narrow we can only crawl one by one. I feel my way in the darkness, carefully placing one hand in front of the other, the rock warm against my palms. The drip drop of water sounds somewhere close by. A cool breeze blasts against my face, surprising me— the freshness tingling the skin on my cheeks. I inhale the fresh damp air. One long deep breath brings my dry throat relief—like breathing in freshly cooled air, damped by rain on a hot summer's day.

Eventually the tunnel opens out into a much larger and cooler space and we are no longer confined to crawling. I slide down a short distance onto a cave floor and my eyes start to see beyond the blackness for the first time.

Above us the tiniest specks of daylight peek through the blackened rock, providing enough light so I can make out the faces of my friends once more. Springing upwards from the floor jagged rocks litter our path, twisting their way into peaks so their tips almost meet the rock above.

From above yet more jagged rocks twist their way back down to the floor, like icicles dripping water from their tips to splash in puddles beneath. The rock icicles are wet to the touch and the stifling heat we've experienced since entering Rubers Law has diminished.

The peculiar nature of the cave means we must weave and squeeze ourselves, one by one, between the jagged rocks. Even though we are small there is little room to manoeuvre. From ahead comes the sound of rushing water and a tunnel, larger than the previous, breaks away from the cave. There before us is a giant waterwheel that churns and clunks, splashing the water down a narrow river, no bigger than a trickling stream to those of normal size, but a frothing, raging river to us. This torrent runs steeply downwards beyond view into the darkness.

'This way?' Jenny questions unsurely, peering down the tunnel.

'Ladies first,' Fie says, with a mischievous glint in his eye as he winks at Jenny, 'I know how you like to swim.'

'Such a gentleman,' Jenny replies winking back. Just as she is about to jump into the river Jimmy steps in front of her. Fixing a glare at Fie he says, 'I will go first. How do we know what's down there?'

'Little brother, I can take care of myself and well you know it,' Jenny says. But Jimmy has already jumped into the water and the rush of the river sweeps him out of sight.

'Here goes! Let's think of this like sledging down a snowy hill at Crossmount,' I say, as I take hold of Jenny's hand and we jump into the river together.

The water feels warmer than I expected yet not nearly as hot as a bath warmed by the fire. Waves quickly rush over my heavy skirt and weigh it down, so I'm immediately pulled ahead of Jenny. The rush of the water is so loud in my ears that it silences my scream as I lose grip of her hand. This is no sledging at Crossmount I think.

With no way to control how fast I am travelling I find myself helplessly lying flat, my arms pushed over my head with the force of the water that bubbles and froths over my mouth. Faster and faster I slide into the darkness. Are we to drown? What a blithering fool I've been to jump so blindly without a moment's thought.

Will this be my last moment? Tumbling helplessly over the most violent of waterfalls. All I can do is try to gulp in the air as the frothy waves ride over my face again and again. I slide side to side, my stomach churning with the rocking motion. If I didn't fear so much where the water ends it might feel exciting to slide and bump along the riverbed.

The water rushes around bend after bend, the current flowing stronger and stronger. All at once my body is bashed against an unexpected turn in the river and my head hits hard against the rock. I'm stunned by the shock of it, my temple throbbing. I can no longer focus my eyes and have to close them. Darkness engulfs me. There's nothing I can do but let myself be pushed further under the flowing water, my head throbbing in time to the waves washing over my face.

WHOOSH!

Suddenly I'm catapulted out into the air, the ground falling from beneath me. I'm flying helplessly in darkness, my arms thrashing wildly above my head as if to grasp for something to steady my fall. It is a relief to plunge back into the water, softening my fall from what seems like a great height. Yet I still find myself wrapped in a fear I cannot escape.

Back under the water I'm pulled further down into terrifying blackness. I open my eyes, desperately searching for the water's surface. It is then I see it—the pale white skin of a hand reaching down to me in the darkness. I reach and grab it, kicking my legs with what little bit of strength I have left.

The pain of the first gasp of air to hit my lungs makes me cry out and I find myself falling backwards, exhausted, into Jimmy's arms. We swim to the edge of the water and stumble onto the rocks.

'You are hurt Wynn,' he says breathlessly, dabbing the bloody gash on my forehead with his sleeve. Blood trickles down my nose and into my mouth, the taste of it like metal on my tongue. I cough and splutter. Jimmy places a hand behind my head and gently guides me so I'm lying down flat against the rock. The throbbing of my wound has faded into a numbness, and dizziness now swirls about my head. As my eyes close I fade into darkness.

'Wynn, wake up, Wynn,' a voice mumbles softly somewhere above, but I can't make out who is calling nor can I respond to them. Slowly I open my eyes to see a small fire lit beside me and my friends staring down at me, the look of greatest concern on their faces. A wet lick against my cheek brings a smile to my face.

'Hey boy, you went for a swim too?' I say to Vargo, so relieved to see his wet black nose poked against mine, his wagging tail flicking water all around. As I sit up, I immediately feel dizzy and have to lie back down for fear of fainting again.

'You hit your head on the way down,' Jimmy says. 'We were worried.'

'I'm well now,' I say. 'Where are we?' As I manage to sit up for a second time, I look around to see we are in another cave, the black rock all around us. Even for us small folk it is relatively small—a mere pocket of air to normal-sized folk. Beside me is a pool of water, the steam rising from its surface.

'Here, eat something,' Jimmy says, handing me a crust of bread, soggy from its journey down the river.

'Thank you,' I say as I gladly take it from his hands. Fie hands me his leather water bottle and I glug the lukewarm water just as greedily.

As the sparks from the fire cackle and flicker light across the cave walls, I shiver and hug my knees to my chest. I can think only of meeting my grandmother Deablin. What will I say? How will I ever be able to look upon my dear friends again if the curse cannot be broken?

I look up. Jimmy sits silently by my side, staring at me. 'Why such a furrowed brow lass?'

Do I tell him my worries when he has so many of his own? Would it be right to add one more?

'What if there's no way to reverse the curse? The moon folk said we'd not find the end of our journey as we expect it,' I say, the sound of the words leaving my lips surprising me.

'Do not worry lass. What will be will be. If it's true our journey is already written in the stars not one of us can change it. Besides, I think back to how we were at Smailholm. Well I think we will be just fine as we are,' Jimmy says, as he reaches for my hand and rests it in his. He is hesitating and biting his lip, just the way he always does when he's nervous and about to say something he's kept buttoned up inside.

'You are perfect, Wynn,' he says, his cheeks blushing a hot rosy red. 'Maybe I didn't realise that before. All these times we've been together, even though we were so different in size, I didn't see you. I am a fool for it. For the shock of nearly losing you just now made me see you for who you really are. This funny, clever girl who I'd be lost not knowing.'

I blush too at Jimmy's honest words and feel the now familiar butterflies flutter in my belly.

'May I hug you?' I say, nervously.

'Of course, I'd like that very much,' he says, and he reaches over until I feel the warmth of his body against mine. His arms pull tightly around my waist and I nestle my head in the nape of his neck. As the fire light flickers, over in the corner of the cave, I catch the eye of Jenny who smiles in my direction. I look away embarrassed.

Lifting my head up from Jimmy's shoulder I find myself boldly looking into his eyes. He cups his hand gently under my chin and slowly pulls me towards him and our lips touch for the first time. My first time. It is strange at first for I'm not really sure how to kiss him back. I must admit it is not how I imagined my first kiss to be. It feels a little awkward and I concentrate so hard on where my lips should go. As our wet lips slip and slide over each other I can feel our teeth suddenly clink together. We break apart and Jimmy laughs.

'Perhaps we need to keep practising,' he says with a confident smile that surprises me.

'Have you kissed anyone before?' I ask, but I can already see how his eyes fall from mine that perhaps he has, and I picture another girl wrapped in his arms.

A jolt of jealously burns through me, as hot as the scalding water beside me, and I lean over to press my lips, more confidently this time, against his. When we finally break our lips apart, we simply smile at each other, a blush of red on both our cheeks. Mine feel as hot as the steaming pool beside me. We sit silently a moment staring at the fire, unsure what to say to one another.

Before I can think what to say a blood-curdling scream fills the air between us. Then another, and another. One after another the screams come in terrifying short bursts.

'What is that?' I whisper clutching on to Jimmy's arms, our eyes wide in horror. The screams are getting louder and closer. I am so terrified that I bury my head against his chest, desperate to escape the sound. I think my heart might skip a beat, for it is obvious that the screams are from not one person alone but many. The desperate sounds of pained souls echo off the rock face, my bones trembling with the fear of it. Jimmy pulls me tight to him.

After a while, the screams start to soften, replaced by the sound of whispering all around. A thousand whispers in one place. Whispering like the rustle of the leaves in a gentle autumn breeze, barely audible until they grow and grow to the sound of a wild storm. A rustle of unrecognisable words cutting through the silence like the sharpest sword.

In the darkness, the voices come in waves. Pulsing. Shifting. One after the other, filling my ears with their eerie sound. I hear different voices now—some male, some female. Mumbling. Whispering. Taunting us.

Warning us.

To the great families of our land whispers are perhaps the most dangerous weapon of all, for many times a whisper has started first a story, then a war.

Just as abruptly as they arrived, the whispers fade to nothing and we all hold our breath, waiting and expecting another wave of sound to follow. Yet it does not come and my own ragged breath is all I can hear.

Fie carefully takes a rectangular whetstone from his pocket and slides it gracefully along the blade of his sword, sharpening it with the swiftness of such movement. 'The spirits, it seems, are awakened to our presence,' he says.

'Well if there are such spirits, there's not a sword in this land, even one as fine as yours, that can do much about them,' Jimmy says.

'True my friend, though after hearing those screams I for one am not taking any chances,' Fie says.

'What do you think they mean?' I ask.

'A warning perhaps,' Jimmy says.

'The quogs could be playing tricks on us. They must be looking for us. Who's to say it wasn't them?' Fie says.

'Well, spirits or not, I say we are safest here tonight,' Jenny says, as she looks around the darkened cave—lit only by the fire. 'If indeed it is night at all.'

Since we've been in Rubers Law it is hard to get any bearing of time. My eyes are sleepy and I do indeed feel like the blackness of the night's sky is above us, although in the heavy darkness of the cave there's simply no way of telling.

'Do you mind if I talk to Wynn for a moment, little brother?' Jenny says. Before either Jimmy or I can do or say anything Jenny is leading me by the hand to the far corner of the cave. I look back at Jimmy who shrugs his shoulders and for a moment, in the flicking of the firelight—I am sure I catch a shake of his head. As I kneel beside Jenny, out of earshot of the rest it would appear, for the first time I become wary of what might be said.

'I see you and my little brother are more than just friends now?' Jenny asks, knowing of course the answer to what is not really a question. I blush but say nothing, fumbling instead with the seam of my dress, which has started to break apart.

'Wynn you know I love you. I can only imagine what having a sister might be like. I imagine it would be nothing short of what I feel for you. I want nothing more than to see you and Jimmy happy—but perhaps now… well maybe now is not the time to place your heart with another.'

I bite my lip, willing myself not to laugh—after all Jenny has done nothing less with Fie. Instead, I feel anger starting to bubble up inside me.

'How can you say that when you and Fie have…'

'Swam almost naked together?' she interrupts, laughing. 'You don't need to lecture me like my little brother. I'm older than you and…'

'Not by much,' I say, annoyed at the mention of my age.

'No, not by much. Although neither am I the heir to the great estate of Ettrick. I am a lady only because Fie chooses to call me one,' she says, hesitating to look in his direction. 'I'll never be a lady like you Wynn. You must know that you have many expectations upon you.'

'And I should be thankful for that? For being taken away from my family to be placed in some cold, unwelcoming house, like a jester to bow and perform to all at court, and to marry an old man I do not know?' I say, aghast that she would be so bold to bring my obligations up now.

'I can see how it might appear, but what better alternative is there? To live your life farming the land as Jimmy does? To toil and scrape when the earth is no longer fruitful? Well it is not a life I would wish for anyone, especially not my sister,' and Jenny takes my hands in hers, just as Jimmy did moments before.

'Maybe it is a happier life?' I say, tears now brimming in my eyes. 'I came here with you because I wanted a happier life for us all.'

'I know you did Wynn and come what may we will never be able to repay your kindness. You must believe that. Even though I know my brother is less sure of which destiny he will choose,' Jenny says as she looks over warily at Jimmy who has turned his back to us.

'I don't want repaying Jenny. I just want to be free, free as the birds above. Just like you.'

'Ah well you see, I'm not sure any lady is free,' she says, her eyes cast downwards.

An awkward silence falls between us. My cheeks burn. I think back to my uncle's words before I left Smailholm. 'You must do as your family bids.' Now I find myself being told once again how to act and what to do—by a friend at that. Am I not able to think for myself? Am I not to be trusted with my own destiny? It seems everyone must think for me—

I will not have it.

'You are not my mother, Jenny!' I say, rage burning my cheeks red.

Jenny looks up, surprised. 'Wynn, wait. I didn't mean... I was just trying to—'

But I am no longer listening, and I turn my back and

stomp away with her words whispering and burning from my ears all the way down to my chest. My skirt, still damp and heavy from the water, weighs my legs down and I stumble past Jimmy. He holds his arm out to catch mine, but I pull away and stomp over to sit next to Fie, who is still sharpening his sword.

Vargo stirs from his slumber at the side of the fire and comes to settle on my feet, the warmth of his dry fur cuddling my toes. I lean down and hug Vargo tight to my chest. I look across the pool and see Jenny and Jimmy exchanging hushed whispers—until I hear Jimmy shout at his sister 'You said what?' and he picks up a rock and throws it into the steaming water, angrier than I've ever seen him.

He disappears into the darkness at the other side of the cave where the flickering light from the fire does not reach. I close my eyes, wishing for the darkness to wash over me and willing the whispering in my head to stop. Eventually I fall into a fitful sleep.

DEABLIN

Thee have come my sweet son. I can see thee now. Am I dreaming that thee finally stand beside my bed? For all these years I dared not hope thee would come—yet here thee are.

Wait! Who stands beside my bed if it is not thee? A young girl? Her eyes the same as thine. Who speaks so quickly I cannot understand. Wait. I can see thee now. Anne-Wynn thee say, a daughter to Thomas Hoppringle.

My. Sweet. Son.

She asks for my help and I will surely give it freely to thy daughter, sweet son. A tale of sprites. Blasted fool I am for I cannot remember any tale of sprites. 'Tis cruel. 'Tis cruel, this mind of mine.

Thee must warn her Thomas not to stay here. The spirits are close by and watching. I fear they will take her as they take so many now. I know they wait for me. Thee have sent her, my sweet son. I am glad for now I may rest at last.

CHAPTER SEVENTEEN

'Where am I?' I jump to my feet and look around. I realise I am alone. 'Where is everyone?' I shout, the echo of my words bouncing off the cave walls. The fire, well-lit before, is nothing more than dying embers.

'Jimmy, Vargo!' I call, stumbling almost blindly from one part of the cave to the other until I realise there is no one here. The darkness is all consuming, the occasional drip of water interrupting an otherwise eerie silence.

Where are they?

I use my hands to feel along the cave walls. Eventually, I come to a small opening. A tunnel perhaps? As I look down it, a sudden draught of warm air blasts against my skin. The heat smothers me and I inhale deeply seeking fresher air, but there is none. Only darkness.

Have they gone this way? I pull my hair from the back of my neck to cool me and crawl forward on my hands and knees. I feel an overwhelming need to turn back yet I know I must continue. Something tells me so. An unspoken voice in my head urges me on.

As I crawl the tunnel narrows until there is only enough room to pull myself along using my elbows. There is no light to guide me. Only darkness. With each movement forward the heat intensifies. Have they been taken? By the quogs? My jaw clenches with the effort of trying not to scream.

'Wait what's that?' I say, whispering to myself. Just ahead there's a tiny pin prick of light. So dim is the light that it flickers on and off, making strange shadows on the rock face, like a candle buffeted by the wind. This first sign of light in an empty darkness offers me some comfort and I crawl towards it. Strangely, as I do so, the light appears to move away. Every time I pull myself further along, the light moves further away until finally it disappears and darkness engulfs me.

I stop to wipe my brow, exhausted from the effort of pulling myself along with my elbows. Surely it is better to stay here awhile? My belly pressed against the warm rock beneath and my head resting on my arms. I feel so tired and alone. The panic rises in my throat with each ragged breath, for I realise how trapped I am in this place.

How could they leave me alone? Wiping the tears from my cheeks with my sleeves, I tilt my head upwards and search out light. Any light to comfort me. Yet it is not blackness I see this time but an intense warm yellow glow that hovers around me, like the warmest fire on the coldest of nights. There directly in front is a sole candle flickering. How peculiar to find a candle so randomly placed, with no indication as to what person or creature might have put it there. I pick up the candle, its presence comforting me when all around is so dark. Crawling forwards, I squeeze myself out through a narrow opening and into a much larger tunnel, lit with candles all along its length. It is such a relief to stand up straight.

Against the other tunnels that we have passed through, this one is much larger, its walls and ceiling carved smoothly from the rock. Beneath my feet hand-made flagstones, just like those in the Great Hall at Smailholm Tower, lead the way in either direction, and every few steps, high upon the wall, a lit candle lights the way. First, I look in one direction, then the other.

Which way?

Turning to my left I start to walk, hesitating every few steps to check what might be in front of me. My feet ache and the stifling heat makes my eyelids heavy. I hesitate, feeling a sudden gust of wind rush from behind. The candles flicker above and beyond, down the tunnel. I freeze for I sense there is something standing right behind me. I'm surprised at how fast my heart is beating. At first, I only hear a low whisper in my ear—one that could almost be dismissed as the rustling of the wind. The second time it is loud enough for me to hear it is indeed the soft voice of a man. It is no whisper. I am most definitely being followed.

'Come with me, my lady,' the voice says.

I hear my own voice in my head. Wynn. Wynn. Wynn—you must be brave and turn around.

'Who summons me, sir?' I say, slowly turning around to see two figures standing silently before me. I can see these figures, yet barely make them out at all. Perhaps they do not even exist. Maybe it is just my mind playing tricks on me. In any case, what I see now are not earthly creatures, however strange. They are something else entirely.

In front of my eyes stand a man and a woman—as ordinary as might look any man and woman—except, just like the candle I hold, their bodies flicker in the light. I realise I am staring mouth agape, half-caught between fear and curiosity—mesmerised by a ghostly presence that is neither here nor there, in this world nor the other.

I look curiously upon their physical form that sure enough appears before me, yet so translucent are their bodies I can see right through them to the tunnel beyond. I suspect if I were to place my hand in theirs I wouldn't feel a thing.

The woman is dressed as our servants might do at Smailholm Tower—an ankle length dress, apron and plain bonnet upon her head. A simple pin clasps a heavy shawl to her breast, falling from her shoulders to just below her waist. The man carries himself nobly, his attire befitting a gentleman of some standing, a billowing shirt nipped at the waist and calf-length trews. He too wears a long heavy cloak draped over his shoulders.

I'm reminded of something my mother once told me when I woke crying from a nightmare filled with ghostly visions. As she stroked my brow to soothe me and whispered words of comfort softly in my ear she told me that when we die our souls must go on a journey to heaven. Sometimes, she said, a soul gets caught between this place and heaven and becomes nothing more than a ghostly version of itself.

I think perhaps they might be able to read my thoughts because, as if to quell my fear, the woman suddenly steps forward, bends down and whispers softly in my ear.

'There is nothing to fear ma lady. We have been expecting you,' she says, a common drawl to her accent.

I imagine the confident greetings my mother gave visitors to Smailholm Tower and reply curtly, 'Whom may I ask has been expecting me?'

'Well ain't she a funny one? All prim and proper for such a young un,' the woman cackles, as she tosses her head back and turns to look upon the man, only to find her joke not shared, a deathly stern expression staring right back.

'Manners!' the man scolds, to which the woman immediately lowers her eyes and stares at her feet. Turning back to address me, the man gently bows his head and says, 'I must apologise my lady, what we have here is nothing more than a scullery maid who has no place in speaking to you in such a way. Please follow me. I will take you to meet your grandmother. Deablin has been waiting for you.'

'Deablin? How does she even know I—'

'Oh, Deablin has been waiting some time for visitors,' he says.

'I don't understand? How could she know I was coming?' For even I didn't know I was coming here myself.

'Please my lady. It is best you speak alone with Deablin. Follow me,' he says authoritatively.

I fear to challenge him again, and he turns to the woman and dismisses her with a flick of his hand, 'You have duties to get to, room III has just rung the bell for assistance.' She nods obediently and bows her head as she walks straight past me and down the tunnel and into the darkness.

I follow the man further into the tunnel and I notice that with every few steps we pass a rounded wooden door, shut fast against the rock face. On each door is a number—V, VI, VII… To the side of each door, carved into the cave wall, are much smaller hatches held fast with an iron latch. Just as I'm passing one such opening, I observe the latch lift, the small door flinging open and banging loudly against the side of the rock to reveal a darkened room beyond. I am so startled by the noise I jump backwards only for the sound of an ear-piercing scream to fill my ears. The scream is shortly followed by a cackle of laughter, womanly in nature, and then the strangest, loudest singing.

'Lyth and lystyn gentilmen. All that nowe be here. Of Litell Johnn that was the knightes man. Goode myrth ye shall here.'

As the man continues to walk ahead, I stop for a moment to listen to the singing and lean forward to peer inside the opening. It is curiosity not bravery that drives me to look. Inside, I can see a small room carved from blackened rock. To one side is a small bed and a stool on which sits a flickering candle. Just as I stretch my neck to peer in further the wild blue eyes of a woman appear and stare right back at me, making me stumble backwards. Startled, I drop the candle at my feet which immediately snuffs out. In the dim light of the tunnel I listen as the woman whispers to me.

'Hello my child, 'tis a long time since I looked upon such a pretty face,' she says, pushing her face up against the hatch. Her crooked hands and long nails clutch at her face and pull at the long white hairs which sprout from her top lip. She tips her head to one side and looks upon me with a dead, glassy stare. I see her shake her head, as if unsure what to say. Indeed, her mouth moves to say something, yet she seems to find no words.

'My lady, we must be quick. You have little time with us I fear,' the man says, as he takes his place by my side once more. He walks towards the small opening and the woman shrinks back into the darkness. Suddenly, out of the hatch an apple core flies right through the man's ghostly body and lands at my feet.

'Lyth and lystyn gentilmen. All that nowe be here,' the woman sings while the man carefully closes the small hatch and replaces the latch.

'Edith likes to sing. Please do not be afraid. Her mind is not what it once was. Please after you,' he says, as he raises his arm and indicates for me to follow.

'We have many residents here. Some, like your grandmother, have been with us for many years. We do our best to take care of them. This is where our residents like to sit a while,' he says, pointing to a small opening cut back into the face of the tunnel. Huddled inside on a pair of rocking chairs are two old men. They rock back and forth. Back and forth without stopping once to look at me. Both wear simple white gowns that fall loosely over their thin bodies. Draped over their laps are beautifully woven blankets, decorated, I observe, with the finest needlework. Their faces, gaunt and pale, stare blankly at a small fire that flickers and spits at their feet.

'Are they not hot?' I ask.

'When old age grows in our bodies my lady, so does our need for warmth.'

I point to a small table next to the men. On it sits a golden jug and two wooden cups. 'Please may I drink the water?' I say, as I pull at the collar of my dress, my tongue so dry it sticks against the roof of my mouth.

'Of course, my lady,' and the man walks over and pours some water, offering it to me. I gulp it back greedily.

The man is so barely there at all I'm afraid he might disappear altogether before my eyes, yet he fills a second cup which he carefully places at the lips of the old man. The man licks at the water, barely moving his head as he does so; only a flicker of his eyes recognising the pleasure of its taste. He coughs and splutters and his hands grip tightly around the arms of his rocking chair, where he shortly settles back to stare blankly at the fire once more. The man's crooked hands rest weakly against the arms of the chair, his skin stretched so thinly over his bones it is almost translucent in appearance—I wonder how someone so thin can still be alive.

'Who are they?' I ask, afraid in part to hear his answer.

'These are great knights of our land, my lady. They bravely fought in many battles. They rest here a while until they are summoned to another place.'

'Where are their families?'

'It is hard to say. Some have no families. Some are forsaken for some shame or other. It is sad to say. It is our penance you see, before we too can move to another place,' he says, sadly.

I look at the two old men and as I do so one briefly stirs, leans across and pulls away the blanket of the other. The man cackles with a triumphant laughter as he grips the stolen blanket tightly to his chest.

'Now, now that is Gereth's blanket. We mustn't take it must we?' the man says, as he gently tugs it from the thief's hands so that it slips off his lap to the floor. I kneel, pick it up and carefully place it back on the lap of the great knight. His glassy gaze momentarily meets my eyes and from the corner of his mouth I notice the glimmer of a smile. Brief though the smile is, for he quickly returns to rocking mindlessly back and forth in his chair.

'Thank you, my lady. I sense you have a great kindness in your heart,' the man says.

I nod, quietly following him in silence. We walk through the tunnel that arcs round until we come to a huge oak door bearing the number VIII.

'My lady I will need to leave you here. Deablin is waiting for you inside,' and the man points at the door before disappearing before my very eyes. I look about me, but nothing remains other than a grey translucent mist that drifts along the tunnel until finally it too disappears.

'Wait...' I shout into the emptiness, but the only answer is the echo of my own voice.

DEABLIN

Shh be quiet I say! Is that a tap at my door? For now,
she stands before me. She takes my hand, pulls the
sheet upon my chest. So kind her gentle hands. Like thine,
my dearest sweet boy.

Ah the sprites—I see them now beneath the Tower
running. Wait, was it I who cast the rain of dust upon
them? She tells me so. My memories drift away from me,
so hard it is to know them. I must find the stones I kept,
where could they be? Damn my mind for hiding them so.

Ah yes, there. As she strokes the hair behind my ears
my comb falls lose into my hands. I have not seen it for
so long, or perhaps not thought to notice it. So beautiful
it is, the finest, blackest stone of all Rubers Law. I take
my fingers and run them over the gilded frame, one stone
gone, the other two remain. A gift to her—as my mother
gifted it to me.

What is done cannot be easily undone. To turn the
curse of sprites to back from whence they came I must

in turn leave this place. Even then only those who want it will normal-sized become. Still now thee have sent a message from home I can finally rest, for I am tired of this place.

Are thee there, sweet son? The darkness so surrounds me now. *Be careful child for every change comes with a price. Shh. For the spirits are coming.* For now, I remember what that first stone took from me. Thy love, my sweet son. *Be gone with thee child!*

CHAPTER EIGHTEEN

I turn to look at the door. Do I knock? Well that surely would be polite, yet what monster will be waiting for me beyond those walls I dare not imagine. Oh, how I wish Jimmy and Jenny were here. No fear would run through Jenny's veins, I am sure.

Steeling all my courage, I tap lightly at the door and push it open. It is much heavier than I imagined. I need to push with both hands, pressing all my weight against it before it moves. As I squeeze through the small opening, flickering candlelight dances across the rock walls.

The small room is sparsely decorated. It has simple rock walls and a stone floor. To one side is a plain wooden bed and a small three-legged table, much like a milking stool, with a candle, a golden jug and wooden cup upon it. The only natural light is from a smattering of tiny small holes etched into the walls. These provide a sprinkling of sunlight from outside and make the dust, that lies heavy in the air, dance in the light.

At first, I do not see the small figure resting on the bed, curled as it is so tightly under a thin white sheet. As I walk closer I see the figure is that of a woman—long wiry grey hair drapes over her face and down to the stone floor. She begins to stir; her twisted hands slowly parting her hair. Two angry turquoise eyes emerge to stare unblinking at me. Her eyes are so piercing that I instantly recognise my own in them and know for sure I am looking upon my grandmother Deablin.

She lies so crookedly upon the bed, twisted and bent out of all normal shape, that it is hard to make out whether her body faces me or not. I stand in silence and watch as she untwists her arms from beneath the sheet and her long dirty finger points directly at me.

'Deablin?' I whisper, quite unsure of what to say or do next.

'Thee forgot about me my child. All of thee!' she scolds, straightening her body so that it lies flat upon the bed and turns her head at the strangest of angles to look upon me. I wonder how it is that she hasn't snapped her neck.

'Thee forgot about me I tell thee!' Deablin says. Her words carve through the heat of the room like ice, scolding me once more. 'I have waited many years for my family to come—and thee say nothing. Speak child! Do you have nothing to say?'

'I...' is all I manage, stuttering over my words and stepping back, for I am most definitely frightened of her.

'Ha!' Deablin cackles. 'I see I make you afraid. Good! For it is thee who should now be afraid, as I have been for many years in this wicked place.'

'Are they not gentle to you?' is all I can think to say.

'Ha child. Thee are as foolish as thy father I see. Gentle? Thee are easily tricked by our ghostly servants,' she says. 'I know you can see them too.'

Her words break off into a tremor. Suddenly, from the corner of my eye I see a speck of light travel into the room. The grey light dances about my eyes, so drawn to it am I that I can look at nothing else. It moves in front of me, growing larger and larger, until finally it takes the form of the ghostly man. He turns and speaks directly to Deablin.

'What seems to be the problem, my lady?'

'Nothing. Away with thee,' but her strong words do not disguise the obvious tremor in her voice as she pulls the bedsheet up to her nose so that just her eyes peek out. I sense nothing but fear in this room. Hers and mine.

'I'm afraid your grandmother can be difficult at times,' the ghostly man says, letting out a sigh as if her lack of obedience irritates him. 'We do our best, of that you can be sure. I shall leave you alone for now and will return shortly,' and just as before he dissolves into a grey mist and disappears. I turn to Deablin and notice a flicker of fear in her eyes.

'Thee have met Brough I see?' Deablin whispers from beneath the sheet. 'He is a rat I say. A filthy, stinking man who has no place tending to a great lady of the court.

Brough told me once he served under my father as one of his chief horsemen. Born into the stables and died in them. Filthy, stinking stables. Murdered by his own brother he was!' she cackles louder now at her own strange tale. 'I know thee see him too. Thee have the same seeing eyes as I. As my mother before me.'

'Why are you here?' I ask, desperate to distract her from her cursing.

'I was put here by my husband—your grandfather.' Deablin shouts, her voice filled with anger until she is sitting almost upright in the bed, jabbing her finger at me. 'Ashamed of me he was so he thought he'd hide me away, like all the other lost souls in this place. These walls are nothing but a prison I tell thee. Thee best watch out you keep your seeing eyes a secret. Or else!'

I do not know what to say to calm her anger, so I say the only thing I can, the only thing I can think of right now, 'I must speak with you and ask you for your help. I came here to ask you to help my friends. To release them from the curse you put upon them.'

'Ha! So it is thee now who want something from me. 'Tis always been the Hoppringle way. What pleasure will it give thee to help these small folk? They are nothing but fools who speak ill of me. Some have even stolen from us. I am sure of it. Of course, your grandfather did not believe me.' She shakes her head furiously, as if searching to say something else now lost to her, until finally she seems to calm and says, 'No matter—what is done is done.'

'But they are my friends. They do not hurt us and they work hard in the fields, like any other. All they seek now is to be released from the curse. They seek to live a peaceful life without the need to worry of what danger might cross their path,' I say, angry thoughts bristling in my head.

'Friends! Thee look upon no friends my child. They whisper about me and wish me ill.'

I watch as she pulls her crooked fingers through her long grey hair and twists the ends around her dirty fingernails. So bitter and twisted, I see nothing but hatred flash in her eyes.

'They are the kindest people I know and no thieves. You have not looked upon them for many years. I see no ill will in them—only kindness. Set them free and be at peace.'

'I will do as I please!' she laughs. 'Thee are a foolish child for that is certain,' and her mad laughter starts to choke her. She wheezes and splutters for breath, doubled over, her hand clutched to her throat.

I step forward and pour water from the jug by her bedside and gently lift the cup to her lips. She grasps it, gulping and gasping down the cool draught that finally settles her coughs. As we look upon each other with the same turquoise blue Hoppringle eyes, I am certain I will see some kindness returned. Her hand slips from her neck, she falls backwards in exhaustion on the bed and I pull the sheet that is twisted around her thin body and settle it gently upon her.

'Thee are kind my child, it is gladly received. For there is little kindness in this place. Do not let those who wander these tunnels so silently deceive you. They appear kindly at first but there is a twist to their presence, and a dark one at that.' She grabs my wrist with her hand and pulls me close to whisper, 'Go child from this place, it is not safe.'

'Grandmother, may I call you that?' I say, watching as she silently nods, a look of mild contentment upon her face. 'I cannot leave, nay will not leave without the promise I made to my friends. The curse has cast a long dark shadow over our land. If our family name ever meant anything to you, please help me now.'

Suddenly, she lifts her hand towards my hair, threading her fingers through my loose curls.

'I used to have these curls, a long time ago of course. A woman's beauty is carried for many years in her hair.' She lifts her hand up behind her head and a jewelled comb falls loose into her hand. She runs her fingers across two black jewels. There is a space between them where a third should be. 'My mother gave me this comb, and her mother to her before that. It is mined from the belly of Rubers Law and the gems carry with them a power which can be used by those who have the same gift as you and I. I used it once at Smailholm—see there is one stone missing. It is thine to use now.'

'But how do I use it grandmother?'

'First thee must decide what thee must lose,' she says, before sitting up in her bed as if a great fear has suddenly gripped her. 'Thee must be quick for they are watching now,' she says and her eyes wander suspiciously around the room. Finally, as if she is sure that no one can hear her, she whispers, 'Be careful child, for every change comes with a price.'

She takes her finger and puts it silently to her lips 'Shh,' she whispers, 'for the spirits are coming.'

Sure enough, the familiar grey mist creeps out from the darkness and twirls around the hem of my dress. As I look back to my grandmother I see she still has hold of the cup, and before I can say anything else I feel the splash of cool water against my skin.

'Be gone with thee child!' she shouts.

DEABLIN

Do not be afraid dear child, for whilst thee show your fear so willingly, finally I have none. Now thee have come and I am now at peace. I close my eyes for they are weary. Worry, fear, nor boredom bother me now.

At last out of the darkness she appears, flying high above the Tower. I can see her now. Sweet Aquila, stretching her wings and hovering on the wind. Flying free. Let me follow thee.

I will see thee granddaughter, perhaps another day.

CHAPTER NINETEEN

Blinking my eyes in the darkness, I search for light. Suddenly, I'm aware of dampness on my face. I jolt awake, realising that it is the familiar wetness of Vargo's tongue licking against my cheek. I am back in the cave and Jimmy is standing over me, offering his hand to lift me to my feet.

'You had a nightmare, lass. You were thrashing about and shouting as the dream took hold of you.'

'It was so very real, Jimmy,' I say, looking around at everyone's wide-eyed stares. The fire beside me is still spitting and burning—just as it was when I closed my eyes.

'You were asleep for a long time,' Fie says, as he pokes at the fire with the last remaining log, 'but now we need to find a way out of this cave.'

I cannot make sense of it at all. As I place my hand upon my hair my fingers brush against something sharp. I pull the object out of my curls and look down upon it.

'It cannot be,' I say. For there in my hands is Deablin's jewelled comb—with one black gem missing from the line of three. As I run my fingers across the two remaining stones I wonder how it can be that a dream is so real to my touch. If the comb in my hand is real then perhaps my dream was too? Have I already met my grandmother? As the questions whir around my head and an uneasy feeling tightens my chest I find myself struggling to breathe, to do anything, like the last wisp of air has been knocked from my lungs. How can this be?

'Wynn? Are you well?' Jenny says, as she places her arms gently around my shoulders.

'I've just had the strangest dream,' I say, not knowing what else to tell her after our vexed words earlier. Words that seem to matter so little now. At least I think it's a dream, I think to myself.

'What did you see?' Jenny asks.

'I… I can't make sense of it,' I say, still clutching the comb tightly in my palm. As I place my other hand against the warm damp rock walls to steady myself—it's then I feel it, a trickle of water running over my hand. I quickly place the comb back in my hair and stand up.

'What the…?' Fie shouts, rising to his feet in panic.

Within seconds our feet are soaked. Water has started to fill the cave, a gushing torrent from an opening in the rock face above us. It quickly extinguishes the fire and total darkness consumes us. But I can feel it. The water rising above my ankles. Then my knees. Before I know it my skirt is heavy, weighted down by the water in the fabric.

I call out for Jimmy. He grabs my hand and squeezes it tight. 'I've got Vargo,' he says. I reach out blindly and feel a mass of wet fur. He doesn't bark.

The water is raining down on us now, showering my face, until I am gasping for air.

'We need to find a way out,' a voice shouts in the darkness. But the noise as the water rushes past my ears is so loud, I cannot tell who cries out. It is taking all my effort to keep my head above water. Until I no longer can and the water slips over my mouth and nose, my head now fully submerged.

I hold my breath and blink in the darkness. There is only a strange silence. Bubbles of air pop from my nose. I can still feel Jimmy's hand in mind, but we are being pulled apart. The force of the water so strong around me, our fingers, so tightly entwined, pull apart until just the gentle touch of his fingertips slips over mine. I reach out with my other hand to grab him, but there is nothing. He's gone. Vargo's gone. My hand is empty, and I submit to the pull of the water as it carries me on its unknown journey. I reach out, my hands searching blindly in front of me, for I know I can no longer hold my breath—the pain in my chest screams. I need to scream out.

I open my mouth, expecting the water to fill my lungs. But it does not. Instead my back bashes against the hardness of rock and I cough and gasp in air in big gulps. The calming light of a candle flickers overhead. Eventually the racing of my heart starts to slow, and I take the longest of breaths and sit up.

I am in a tunnel. The same stone floor as my dream. The same flickering candles on the tunnel walls that weave out of sight in either direction. Is this a dream? Am I dead? But there, as I look up, I see an opening into the tunnel I am sitting in, trickling with water.

I touch my hair. It is wet, drenched with a thousand droplets of water. Am I still alive? My heart beats against my chest; my breath shortening. I look around me, down the flickering light of the tunnel to the darkness beyond.

It suddenly occurs to me that I am no longer small because the size of everything around me—the candles, floor and tunnel—seem just as they should. But I am alone. No Jimmy, Vargo, Jenny or Fie. No ghostly spirits. No noise. Just an eerie stillness buffeted by the whistle of the hot wind that sweeps towards me from the long tunnel beyond, flickering the flames of the candles so shadows dance on the rock walls. I don't know what I was expecting when I came back to this strange place, if indeed I've been here before—but it was not silence. I want to call out for Jimmy. Should I? Who, or what, will hear me? I gulp, quelling the rising panic in my throat.

Leaning on the rock wall, I pull myself to my feet. I know the way to go. I've been here before. The sound of my hurried footsteps echoes in the silence. Sure enough, the tunnel quickly arcs round to reveal the opening of the cave where I met the two knights. The last dying embers of the fire smoulder on the ground and the rocking chairs move gently back and forth—empty. Where have they gone? I'm running now, faster and faster, past the candles hung high on the walls that flicker between light and dark. Until I stop and turn to the great oak door, carved with the number VIII.

I can hear them again. The whispers. Louder and louder they whisper in my ears.

I push against the door, discovering a haste in myself that can't quite be explained. I squeeze myself through the gap, entering the dimly lit room beyond. As I turn to look back into the tunnel I find myself suddenly pulled by some unknown force which slams me against the rock face. I watch in horror as the door slams shut and the iron key turns slowly in the latch.

'Thee came my child,' a sombre voice whispers from the gloom.

There before me, just as I had dreamt it so clearly, the tiny figure of Deablin is curled upon a simple wooden bed, her hand extended weakly, beckoning me towards her. I walk over and place my hand in hers, fearful of doing anything else. My heart is beating so strongly I feel every single pound against my chest.

'Do not be afraid child,' she whispers.

'I am not afraid grandmother.'

'You are kind my child, but thee are unwise to walk within these walls.'

'You gave me this gift,' I say, showing her the jewelled comb in my hand. 'What must I do with it to free my friends from this wicked curse?'

'Wicked!' she cackles. ''Tis not wicked child when those cursed spoke so wicked of me. Did thee not listen before to my words? It was a worthy punishment for those fools. Besides no jewel or magic will change what's done. For you must keep the gems to use when you most need them—a deed that only thee can decide upon. Though thee must be mindful of their powers when combined with the gift you were given—for both are strong and can easily change what has been written in the stars.'

'You promised to help me!' I cry, the anguished wail of my words surprising me as it leaves my lips.

'I promised nothing child. But I will tell thee this—for those who want to be set free from the curse will be, but only once I leave this place. For every change has a price.'

'And what price must I pay?' I ask. 'For I will do anything to help my friends.'

'You surprise me with your kindly heart. I see thy father in thee. Do not worry child for I have been waiting for thee. Such a long time I have been waiting—I do believe you have already paid the price, for like I, you carry the second sight. Be mindful of it. It is a gift that so easily displeases others. For everyone fears what they cannot understand.

'Thee have come at last and I am thankful and ready to rest. It will not be long, I hear them creeping in the darkest corners. Do you see them as I do my child? I am ready for them now,' she says as she lays her head back down upon the bed and closes her eyes. 'Be gone with you child, back to Smailholm Tower. Your family are waiting.' Her eyes are still closed, a look of peace smoothing the lines of her face. 'Quickly child, be gone, for they are coming,' she says suddenly, grasping her hand around my wrist. 'They are here again. Can't you hear the whispers?'

I look around the cave room and there in the darkness of corners I see it. The grey mist emerging into the flickering light of the candle. It weaves its way into the centre of the room, twisting its translucent form around the bed until it comes to rest peacefully around Deablin. From the mist appears many hands, barely there at all in any human form, but for all that they grasp at Deablin's clothes—tugging and pulling her this way and that. The hands wrap around her and pull her forward until she is almost sitting up on the bed directly in front of me.

'Grandmother!' I scream. She opens her eyes for one last time and as a ghostly arm wraps itself around her neck she gasps, 'Do not fear what thee see—I am ready to leave this place.' Whereupon, she closes her eyes and I glimpse for a moment peace upon her face—until she is gone, into darkness.

'No, it cannot be so!' I scream. A muffled voice calls my name, accompanied by furious banging against the door. There is only a moment of brief, deathly silence, before the whispering returns; yet now it is beckoning me to follow.

Suddenly the door to the room flies wide open and clatters against the rock wall, free from the strange force that held it shut. Fie and Jenny rush into the room. Jenny wraps her arms around me.

'You are free from the curse!' I say, amazed that they are both now the same size as I. 'Deablin told me that the curse would be broken when she left this place,' I say, hot tears trickling down my cheeks.

'Are you hurt?' Fie asks.

'No, but my grandmother, Deablin, she was taken, I, I…' the words no longer making any sense in my head. 'But Jimmy and Vargo?' I say, 'where are they?' Tears are rolling down my cheeks.

Jenny and Fie stare back at me, dazed, no words to comfort me. 'We believe them gone. In the water. But we are alive Wynn so we must believe they are as well,' she says, pulling me towards her.

My head nestles on her shoulder, seeking comfort in this coldest of moments. I notice from the corner of my eye a speck of tiny grey light appear once more. It quickly grows ever larger, until the very same ghostly hands that took Deablin crawl out into the flickering light. I am frozen in horror as they start to wrap their hands around Jenny and Fie.

'Can't you see them?' I scream.

'See what?' Jenny says, looking calmly around her.

'Can't you hear the noise?' I say, putting my hands over my ears to crowd out the whispers that fill them. The noise so unbearably loud and close, I fear it may sweep me away. I close my eyes wishing it gone. Wishing Jimmy and Vargo to appear.

When I open my eyes again the ghostly hands, wrapped so tightly around Fie and Jenny, reach out to

me. Their translucent fingers move ever closer towards
my face. I know we must leave this place, before it is too
late and they take us all.

'Quickly!' I say, 'we must go, now!' and I grab hold of
Jenny and Fie's hands and pull them out of the cave room
and into the tunnel beyond.

CHAPTER TWENTY

The whispers have stopped. For a moment all is silent. I rest my hand against the rock to support my trembling legs, clawing at its rough surface, a comforting warmth seeping through my palm. An eerie silence settles, broken only by the occasional whistle of wind through the tunnel.

'Wynn?' a voice says. 'Wynn are you well?' I look up and there is Jenny, comforting me as she always does. Braver than I ever could be. But there is a puzzled look in her eyes. 'What is it Wynn?' she insists. 'Why are you so afraid?'

'Where are they?' I ask, my voice trembling.

'We will find them, Wynn. I promise.'

But the knot of grief has grown to a tight coil, so large I cannot ignore it. 'I hope that is true,' I reply, trying to show the strength she does, but for once not really believing her.

I think back to Deablin's warning—that everything comes with a price. Is the price the two who I hold so close to my heart? Or is the price another? Do I tell my friends about the ghostly spirits I can see but they do not? Or has the madness struck me down as it did my grandmother. For I can no longer tell what is real anymore.

'We must search for them,' Jenny says.

'No, we must leave, Jenny. Leave this place,' I say, as a crescendo of whispers gathers pace around my ears once more. The spirits will come back. I know it.

'My brother,' Jenny says, 'I won't leave without him. How could we ever leave without them?'

'We will make a way to find them both again, but our best hope is to get out of here now,' Fie says, with a small nod of agreement in my direction.

As we make our way down the tunnel, not knowing which direction to take, I look back and watch as the ghostly grey mist slowly follows us, seeping silently from the darkness, slinking itself along the tunnel floor until it comes to a sudden stop. Two ghostly hands appear, their shadows dancing on the wall as the candles flicker between light and dark. The hands move backwards and forwards, as if to urge us away, until seemingly satisfied that we won't return, they ease back into the darkness and disappear completely.

As we walk along the tunnel in silence, all seemingly contemplating the horror of our journey from Rubers Law without our friends, I think back to Deablin's warning, and that of the moon folk; that our journey will not end as we planned. Eventually, with the last of the candles marking our way behind us, we come to a fork in the tunnel. As darkness marks our way in every direction Fie sighs, 'Another leap of faith? Which way?'

'This way my friends,' says a familiar voice. There flickering in the darkness is the flame of a single candle carried by the quog king himself with two quogs carrying swords. He waddles towards us on his tiny legs, barely visible under the weight of his enormous belly. 'Though I see you are no longer small,' he squints at us, surprised at our new-found size.

Immediately Jenny takes aim with her bow and arrow at the king quog's head, but this time instead of taunting us, he takes a step back—we are now almost double his size. 'Now, now my lady. Is that any way to greet a friend?'

'You are no friend of mine, quog. What have you done to my brother and Vargo?' she demands.

'Ah, I see you have lost your companions along the way. Such a pity,' he says, looking upon us with ghastly bloodshot eyes that seem to bulge even further from their sockets. 'Alas, Rubers Law is unpredictable. For many this place is the walk between life and death. But you are wrong my lady, there is no reason to fear my kind.'

'You could have fooled me, quog,' Fie says, drawing his sword from his scabbard.

'Now, now, come—we are all friends here and I am of course most humbly at your service,' the king says.

I push down Jenny's bow with my hand, 'So, if we are friends, will you help us?'

'Now let me think, my lady,' he says, unfolding one black gnarled claw to scratch his egg-shaped head. After a moment he says, 'The answer will be yes I think, however as with everything in Rubers Law you will find it comes with a price.'

'And what price may that be? For I am in no mood to bargain, sir. This place has cost me dearly already.'

'You have what you came for yes? The curse relinquished. Much to the pity,' the king says. 'Deablin always was a kindly soul. She will be greatly missed.' He stares at me, his bulbous eyes unblinking.

Jenny raises her bow and steps towards the king, her hands gripped so tightly around it her knuckles have turned white.

'Wait,' I say, placing my hand gently on her shoulder. 'What do you ask of us?'

'The adventure you set upon has found you what you craved, 'tis true. I fear though the Rubers Law has got the better of you. Certainly, your friends at least. It is always best to learn from the king in these matters,' he says.

'You are no king of mine. A queen is raised upon this land, not the half-witted, cruel and ugly creature that I look upon now.' Jenny stands defiantly in front of him, her arrow almost touching the tip of his nose.

'Half-witted? Why your words are like a knife to my heart my lady,' and he lifts his arm up dramatically and places three talons next to his heart and bends his head as if to bow to Jenny. 'I am no match for you my lady, 'tis true; half-blind and a body good only for climbing, yet I have ruled over Rubers Law for many years and provide good services to your kingdom. I take many a poor shamed soul and hide them away.'

'Aye and make a pretty penny out of it too,' Fie scoffs.

'Stop, all of you,' and I cup my hands over my ears, longing for silence. All I hear are the whispers gathering again. 'Be quick and tell us what you want?'

'My lady, I will offer those who stand before me the way out of Rubers Law safely. Sadly I cannot promise to return your two lost friends, but I will send my men to search Rubers Law for them. Be they alive or dead I cannot say, yet I will return them to you. There are two conditions to this bargain. The first is that I offer this arrangement now and only now. Quogs by nature are impatient for reward and I am not prepared to wait.'

'And what is the second condition?' I ask.

'Why, you must take me with you,' the king says.

'Take you where?'

'To Smailholm Tower and beyond to where you meet your queen at Traquair. I am told you are soon to be your queen's lady in waiting—is that not true?'

'You wish to come to court?' and I almost snigger at the ridiculousness of the request he has put upon me. 'Do you realise how they will look upon you?'

'My lady, I have many years lived in this kingdom and never been surprised how quickly the eyes of your court are turned by the presence of gold in a quog's pocket,' he says confidently.

'Very well you have your request, although I cannot promise you will be welcomed.'

'No matter, my lady. I will take care of that,' and the king quog, satisfied with his bargain, turns his back on us and waddles into the darkness, until just the flame of the candle he holds flickers ahead. 'Follow me,' he says.

'Well Wynn, it seems you have just made your first quog bargain,' Fie says, taking my hand in his as if to reassure me that I've done the right thing. 'We will find them again Wynn, I promise,' and he squeezes my hand even tighter.

At this very moment, as the grey mist of spirits gathers ever closer around us, I realise I will do anything to leave this place. Fie offers his other hand to Jenny and as she tentatively accepts, we walk side by side through the darkness of Rubers Law.

CHAPTER TWENTY-ONE

As we emerge from the treeline of Ettrick, there on the horizon, Smailholm Tower pierces the morning mist that gathers like a frosted sea on the moor. My heart leaps as I see the Tower and I realise I'm just one more stoop from home. Our journey back has been with speed, just two days in fact. Yet not without toil. Our horses are weak and clumsy and pull at their bits, stumbling over their own hooves—frustrated it seems by their new larger size.

When we emerged from the belly of Rubers Law into the blinding brightness of a foggy day, the vision of our horses beyond the river, normal in size and grazing quietly, filled our hearts with hope that all those at Smailholm had made the same transformation.

I wonder now how it can be that we feel little difference in our own bodies and minds, now that we are large again. It is true that the land and animals around us now seem to sit in harmony with our souls. Yet I am surprised to find my heart misses skipping between the leaves of the forest floor and finding easy places to hide from the creatures of the forest. Fie, the oldest amongst us, says that whilst his body grows strong and tall, his heart feels weak and a little empty from its new place in the world.

It is true that we all feel weak in our stride, for our food from Smailholm has long since gone and the quog king has provided us with meagre supplies for our journey back. For such a wealthy man he travels light with just one horse and two servants. He scoffs as we turn our noses up at what he calls, 'his finest prepared broth of night bugs, frogs and ear worms.'

My thoughts drift back to our night in Luds Stoop, and despite my protestations at the slimy snail stew Jenny had prepared, my mouth now waters at the thought of the very same.

'A welcome sight my lady?' Fie asks, as he gazes upon the Tower.

'It is, Fie,' I say a little unsurely—for I cannot ignore the growing ball of worry in the pit of my stomach. How will I return to such a life? The frivolity of the court at Traquair and my sisters who cannot begin to understand the pieces of my heart that I have lost upon this journey. Jimmy, Vargo—I can only think of them lost now. Will I ever see them again?

I surely hope that mother and father will welcome me back, but what of this strange folk that now accompany us? The king squats smugly nearby, his bulbous eyes feasting on his prize. I can see his eyes have started to fail as he walks in sunlight for the first time in many a year. He squints and blinks as water streams from his eyes down his black furred cheeks, until it finally drips from his rounded chin to a puddle at his feet.

He reaches into the small leather pouch that dangles from his neck and scoops out a handful of what looks like ground dry herbs which he duly sniffs. As the potion takes effect blood red veins start to pulse like tiny flowing rivers over the whites of his eyes. Goodness knows how Smailholm folk will look upon him.

I do observe his servants carry with them all manner of gems as well as extra supplies of the potion he sniffs. I wonder if he will soon grow tired of a court, where he will no longer hold the power he has at Rubers Law, and will instead be looked upon with pity and curiosity. Will the gems he brings be sufficient to buy his way into affections? And what of Rubers Law? Will the quogs still mine the black stone for his gain alone? As the thoughts spin around in my head, I turn towards Jenny.

'Such a strange creature,' she whispers to me, as if reading my thoughts. 'Walking among us as if he rules over this land.' I am happy to hear Jenny's voice for she has barely spoken since we left Rubers Law. Her voice is hoarse and a little broken as she struggles to regain her spirit. For it is lost I think, like mine. Even at the sight of home I do not think I can find it. For neither of us imagined journeying back here without Jimmy or Vargo.

'It looks smaller somehow,' she ponders, 'don't you think?'

'A little.'

'Are you worried?' she asks, 'about how your father will greet you?'

'A little,' and with that the silence drifts between us again, for there is naught else to say. And so I begin walking across the moors towards home.

Finally, we clamber up the rocks towards the barmkin wall of Smailholm Tower and I'm greeted with the joyous noise and smell of market day—a day when the farmers and bakers come from Ettrick and beyond to trade their wares with aplomb.

'Fresh bread baked at dawn, come now for soon it will be gone,' a maid sings heartily. I am so transfixed with the delicious smell that wafts beneath my nose that I shout out to catch Mrs Jetty's attention.

Alas, the maid turns around to answer my friendly call, but looks blankly upon my face—and I realise that although she carries the same weight around her frame, her hearty appearance is that of a younger woman. I'm not sure where I expected the Smailholm folk to go now that their spritely bodies have grown and grown. Part of me is a little disappointed that it is not my old friend. Nor can I see any other folk from Smailholm. Have they not come back to the Tower now that they are normal-sized once more?

'Bread my lady?' she asks.

'I have nothing with which to pay you,' I say.

'Let me,' says the king, who waddles forward confidently and stands in front of the baker maid, placing a fine gold coin upon the palm of her hand.

I can see the same silent scream that once fell upon my lips sits now at the back of her throat, waiting to escape as she looks at the peculiar creature that stands before her. Instead, she closes her hand tightly around the coin, more money I think than she has ever seen in her life, and stumbles out the words, 'thank you, kind sir'.

I wonder how much kindness a gold coin can bring a man, or indeed a creature of any sort. Yet as the farmers and bakers gather around to cast their eyes upon the king and his bulging pockets of gold, hearty laughs and friendly greetings are exchanged. I think, perhaps, gold can buy you a lot.

No matter now, as my thoughts turn quickly back to the warm bread in my hands—which we readily share between us. We each in turn place the bread against our nostrils and sniff deeply the intoxicating smell of wheat and rye, fresh from the fields of summer and ground down to the softest, sweetest taste I can ever remember.

As I hastily gobble down the last of the bread I happen to look upon the open door to the Tower and see a figure of a man placing a hand against the frame, as if to prevent a stumble from knees which have become weak at the joints. As I look upon his face I see tears running down his cheeks, catching light from the sun that has peeked momentarily from the grey clouds.

'Wynn! Wynn! Do my eyes deceive me? For I have searched these moors every night. 'Tis true my hope was wavering,' and he rushes to me and gathers me in his arms so tightly I gasp for breath. 'Wynn is it really you my child?'

'I'm sorry father, so sorry,' and knowing those are the only words I can say, I bury my head in his chest and sob until my tears run dry.

CHAPTER TWENTY-TWO

I pull at the tight collar of the dress that mother has insisted I wear tonight for the feast that has been hastily arranged to mark my safe return. I am pleased to see her so, her sweet scent filling my nostrils as I bury my face against her shoulder, reminding me that I am once again home. Mother and father are full of questions, and mostly I have left them unanswered, a growing shadow between us I fear, for their questions are too difficult to find a reply.

They watch me from across the room, as they have done since I returned, in fear of leaving my side. Since arriving back a few hours ago, I have not wished to talk much. My greetings, even to my sisters, have been brief and inadequate, and I have done what I could to avoid their questioning gaze. Mother and father sensed my discomfort and immediately whisked me away to our chamber where they have watched over me silently since. I have washed and slept for the most part.

I tug at my hair, a frizzy mess of curls that I have been unable to comb properly since I left. 'Let me Wynn,' mother says, taking my comb and delicately undoing each knot in my hair, one by one. 'I have missed you so much Wynn. I thought you were lost my darling child.'

I turn around and smile at her, the guilt sticking at the back of my throat. I do not want more questions arising between us. 'We must make an appearance in the Great Hall, they will be waiting.'

'Soon enough my darling, your sisters wish to see you first,' mother says, as she strokes my flushed cheeks. 'Look here they are my darling.'

Juju runs across the room to greet me, swiftly followed by Anne.

'We will leave you in peace. But don't spend too long blathering,' mother says as she and father leave our chamber.

'Wynn, Wynn, we've been desperate to speak to you. Mother said you needed rest,' she says excitedly throwing her arms around my neck. 'We have much to tell you!'

'For goodness sake Juju, let go of the poor girl,' Anne says, as she takes my hand warmly in hers. 'I dare not ask where you have been, we are just glad to have you home safely.'

'Poor you—having to travel with that ghastly creature,' Juju says. 'They say he rules over Rubers Law? Is it true Wynn? Did you visit them? And what of Vargo—that ghastly dog, did he run away too?' She babbles on excitedly, a barrage of questions falling from her lips. I wonder how I can ever begin to answer them.

'It is true dear sister that the quog is the king of that realm, a surprisingly resourceful creature who thinks of nothing more than his own interests—but enough of my adventures, what of yours?'

'Well, mother has promised me she will have made the most wonderful dress for Anne's wedding. She is employing the finest seamstress in Ettrick. She says I may take it to Traquair, as is befitting of a lady at court. She's sent for one for you too Wynn, never losing hope that you may return.'

'Your strange disappearance has been so hard on mother, Wynn. Most days she did not once leave her bed,' Anne says.

'And I hear the wedding is in a week?' I say, ignoring her scornful look.

Before Anne can reply Juju says, 'Yes, it is so lucky that you were brought back to us in good time. We are bursting with excitement. Father has invited every laird from miles around and the greatest feast is to be had. There's to be dancing and merriment until dawn and then the finest carriage in the county will take us all the way to Traquair, where another dance will be laid on for our arrival. I wonder who we will meet, Wynn?' Juju's eyes briefly glaze over with the thought of such adventures. 'There's more, Wynn,' she whispers excitedly. 'The best secret you could ever hope to hear.'

'What is it?' I ask, curious despite myself.

'I can hardly believe it, but Uncle Eanraig has found the most wonderful tiny little sprite. Whilst out riding looking for you he came across a strange tiny woman near Luds Stoop. Hiding in the stoop itself she was! He says she will make him the richest man in the land. At first, we did not believe him, but we have seen her, Wynn, with our very own eyes, and it is true she is a sight to behold. No bigger than my peg doll, yet her voice so loud for she shouts and curses at being trapped in a cage.'

My heart skips a beat and I stand there in silence, mouth agape, fearing to take in the story Juju has just told.

'Wynn, are you well?' Anne asks. 'Your face is very pale. Perhaps you should rest a while.'

I cannot answer for I fear that the only sound to come from my mouth will be a scream. I pick up the hem of my skirt and stumble to the turret steps, cursing the promises made by Deablin. She promised me she had freed Smailholm from her curse, so how could Juju's words be true? To lose Jimmy and Vargo for nothing? It cannot be!

In the Great Hall, Fie and Jenny sit together staring intently into the flames of the newly lit fire. Fie looks up and I smile hopefully, desperate to touch upon the comfort that we once felt together.

He smiles back, his eyes dazed from looking upon the finery he has so long lived without—even though it still befits his family name. Despite his title he has lived without such comfort and now looks a little out of place at his surroundings, as indeed one might think the quog king would do. Yet of the strange band of travellers that have made their way into the safety of Smailholm Tower, the quog king already appears the most at home. I do not know how it is possible for one single creature to receive so much attention yet manage it so well.

He sits alongside Uncle Eanraig, discussing in depth the mining business of Rubers Law and its much-prized gems. A bag of gold coins weighs heavy on his belt— this hasn't gone unnoticed to Uncle Eanraig—nor the crowd that gathers around him, as he regales them with his money-making tales. His jovial cackle echoes loudly throughout the tower so every chamber is aware of his presence.

'Fools! Why do they listen to such a creature?' Jenny asks.

'A piece of gold is why. It shines in the eyes of men and makes them blind,' Fie replies.

I walk over to Uncle Eanraig, desperately trying to regain my composure. I do not want to cause Jenny and Fie alarm at the story I have just been told, for my heart aches with the loss enough without inflicting it on my friends.

'May I speak with you uncle?' I say, and he looks up, a surprised expression on his face.

'Can it wait Wynn? Your friend and I have business matters to attend to.'

'No, it really cannot uncle.'

'Very well, Wynn,' he says. 'Let's discuss this in your father's chamber downstairs. I can collect something I wish to show the king here. A prize to rival any gem in

Rubers Law,' he exclaims, turning towards the king with a gleeful smile that stretches from ear to ear.

The king laughs heartily and signals for one of his servants, who readily presents a small tied pouch in his hand. 'Really, my friend? Indeed, that would be something to see. For my gems are breathtakingly beautiful—are they not?' he says, emptying the contents of the pouch onto the table. As the crowd marvels at the handful of sparkling red gems before them I turn my back quickly. For I know what prize my uncle talks of. And now where it might be!

I run down the steps to the base of Smailholm Tower, where my father's chamber can be found. Knocking quietly on the door I open it tentatively in case he is at work at his desk, as he so usually is, sighing with relief when I realise the room is silent and empty. I pace back and forth, stomping my heels against the stone floor, and clutch my hands together to stop them shaking from the rage that washes over me. Suddenly a voice can be heard in the darkest corner of the room.

'Who's there? Let me out I beg thee!' and I know immediately who calls out for help. Why it is my old friend Mrs Jetty, so recognisable is her tiny voice. There in the dark corner of the room I can just make out a black cloth which lies over some round object. I bend down and pull off the cloth to reveal a gilded cage. Yet it is not this at which I marvel, but the tiny pocket-sized woman that stands looking up at me with the broadest smile spread across her face.

'Wynn, I knew you were not lost! I knew you'd come for us.'

'Oh, Mrs Jetty, I curse my uncle for his stupidity in keeping you in such a horrid place.'

'Wynn we must be quick,' she says.

'Has he hurt you my friend?'

'No Wynn, but he taunts and teases me, pokes and prods to make me dance like a stupid court fool, and you know my knees are not what they used to be. They hurt so from bending down to the oven all these years.

'And bread. He makes me bake bread, buns and the finest cakes on a tiny fire, and amuses himself with how little they are, yet rightly scoffs them down so quickly I can never bake enough for his big belly. My hands are red raw with baking. Look!' She turns her palms upwards and I squint to see them, so small they are, yet I can still see the red marks and blisters upon her palms.

'Quick my lady, I hear his footsteps,' Mrs Jetty says, her voice trembling. So, I open the cage and carefully pick her up, placing her deep in my dress pocket. 'Shh, be quiet now,' I urge her. 'For I will take you back to the safest place I know,' I say, closing the bird cage and placing the cloth back over it so that it appears as if nothing has moved. I jump up as Uncle Eanraig enters and hope that he has not seen how flustered I am.

'Why Wynn, it is a fine day to see you safe and well again. Let me greet you as any man might do to a great lady of the court,' and he reaches over to take my hand and kiss it.

So shocked am I by the touch of his lips against the back of my hand that I grit my teeth, trying not to flinch. I am grateful though he has not yet noticed my flushed cheeks, for I have never been good at hiding mischief.

'And so, what brings you to my door? Do you need to ask a favour of your uncle—my dear niece?'

'This is my father's chamber is it not—not yours?' I say. 'I ask, uncle, that you reconsider my place at Traquair?' I fumble in my pocket as I feel Mrs Jetty squirm against the back of my hand.

'Why dear niece, you cut me so with your words. My door is your father's, and his mine, after all we are all one family,' he says, smirking a little. 'With regards to your soon to be departure to Traquair, I'm afraid it cannot be changed. It is befitting of a lady such as yourself and will earn this family an important place at court. That is surely something you would not begrudge your dear mother and father after your little trip away, so worried have they been I do not think they could take another disappointment.'

'Uncle you are a powerful man, are you not?' I say, watching as he grins in agreement. 'For would a powerful man not earn his family's place at court without the need of assistance from his niece?'

His jaw tenses, a twitch now upon his top lip. He reaches forward and grabs my wrist, yanking my hand from the pocket of my dress. I look defiantly into his glowering eyes, hoping he has not seen my pocket open with Mrs Jetty inside.

He yanks me towards him, his face so close to mine I can feel his hot breath on my cheek. 'Do as you are told Wynn. For you know the stories of Rubers Law? I'm sure your new friend would be happy to take you in,' he says, his hand tightening around my wrist.

I bite my lip to stop myself laughing at his words. Words that once would have scared me, but no longer. I think of the fear that once took hold of my nightmares—fear of the unseen and unknown. Now it is another kind of fear that tightens my stomach. The fear of loss. Loss of my friends—Jimmy and Vargo. And of the tiny woman who hides in my pocket.

I snatch my wrist away from his grasp. 'No matter uncle, I will go to Traquair—but on my father's wish, not yours,' I say defiantly, my teeth clenched in anger. Before he can reply I bolt for the door, and beyond—across the moor towards Smailholm.

CHAPTER TWENTY-THREE

As I place Mrs Jetty safely down into Smailholm marketplace I realise at once it is completely deserted. 'How did my uncle find you at Luds Stoop?' I ask.

'Why child, I was out looking for everyone else. One morn, a few days past, Mr Jetty and I woke to find the village so quiet. Not a soul about there was. After a time, I found Caen the blacksmith and his wife. Mr Smelt too. And a few others that were wandering about scratching their heads about where everyone else had disappeared to.

'The only thing to do was look beyond our boundary. And that's exactly what we did, until I found Flora wandering around in a daze by Luds Stoop. Yet normal-sized she was. When she came to her senses she said she'd awoken on the moor like that with no idea how she got there. There were others too. Of course, they all ran to trees when they saw your uncle's men approaching. I hid in the stoop only for your uncle's men to find me.'

I look down upon Mrs Jetty confused, furrowing my brow at the thought of Deablin's words, until I realise this is what she did indeed tell me—that all those who want to be released from the curse will be so.

'Did you not want to be free from the curse?' I ask.

'Do not worry child, Mr Jetty and I are too long in the tooth for starting our lives anew. We have been this way for a long time and it is rightly so. We have others here to keep us company who have chosen to stay, including Tom and Mr Smelt. Happy as a lark I shall be now that I no longer have to bake so many of those blasted buns,' and she laughs heartily at the thought of her hard-earned retirement.

'I shall miss thee Wynn. Will ye come to visit us from time to time? I have already missed your company—and even that daft dog of yours. Where is the dopey beast?'

'Oh, Mrs Jetty,' I say, bursting into great heaving sobs at the thought of him lost in Rubers Law with Jimmy. 'Why he's gone. They both are and my heart with them.'

'Well my lady, 'tis a sorry state and make no bones about it,' she says, shaking her head in befuddlement. 'I could not have imagined such bad luck, except perhaps the time we all came to be small in Smailholm in the first place. Is there nothing to be done?'

'I made a bargain with the king of the quogs, who says he will help me in exchange for introducing him at court. Yet I do not trust him one bit, and besides I know I must leave for Traquair soon, after my sister's wedding.'

'Indeed, 'tis best not to trust a creature whose pockets lay heavy with gold. I heard your uncle talking to him in your father's chamber just yesterday. Many a business deal they did discuss, that I could not nor did not want to understand—a pair of scheming fiends they both are I suspect. No matter, my lady, you will find a way. Besides look what you've done,' and she points towards the empty Smailholm marketplace. 'For years we've been prisoners in our own small world and even if I did not want it so, you gave a precious gift to all those who've walked these streets. You gave them choice my lady, and that is all anyone can ask.'

'It does not bring Jimmy and Vargo back to me though,' I say.

'Do not cry, my dearest friend, or else my hands will be red again with effort from mopping up your flood.'

I laugh for the first time since I arrived back home.

'By all accounts, the quog king gives some hope. But be careful, my lady you would be well not to trust that strange creature.'

'I see no other way but to trust him now,' I say, before bidding her farewell, my heart heavy with the thought of Jimmy and Vargo so far from home.

As I walk back to Smailholm Tower the sun peeks out from the cold grey clouds and shines warmth on my tear-stained cheeks. Gradually strength returns to my weary limbs and I start to run, faster and faster towards the Tower. For I know that the quicker I accept my own fate, the quicker I may find Jimmy and Vargo.

For the first time since they were lost to me, I know what I must do.

CHAPTER TWENTY-FOUR

As the carriage pulls slowly away from Smailholm Tower, bumping as it does over the rocky earth of the moor, I turn my head to look out of the window and see father waving excitedly. Mother clutches her white handkerchief to her chest, a solitary tear running down her cheek. Juju weeps at the side of me. I reach down and grasp her hand.

'I was so looking forward to going, but I do not know how I will cope without them,' she cries.

'Oh Juju, ever the queen of the performance,' Anne says, as she looks to her new husband Rubin and shrugs her shoulders. I watch as they giggle, foreheads pressed together in a private exchange, as only the newly wedded can do.

Juju sinks back into her seat beside me. I squeeze her hand to reassure her. 'Remember, they will soon arrive at Traquair for the Yule feast, and the Queen herself will come later for a hunting expedition,' I say, watching as Juju's eyes brighten at the thought of such events.

'I wonder if the feast will have the jugglers from your wedding. They were so amusing! Uncle Eanraig's fury was something to behold when one of them bounced a ball upon his nose,' Juju giggles, her tears soon drying at the thought of new adventures.

I think back to the wedding this morn, the Great Hall full to bursting with all the lairds of the county. The music so perfectly chosen, as only mother could have done, its sweet cheerful notes bringing a smile to many a face.

I have never seen father so happy as when he gave Anne's hand to Rubin. Anne was surely the finest maiden to behold on her wedding day. Gliding into the Great Hall with her hair neatly tucked in soft ringlets around her face, held in place by the simplest band of red berries. Many would have said her dress too simple and plain for a lady of Ettrick, yet she carried it finely as only Anne could. The lightest shade of green, it only sought to make her delicate face and turquoise eyes the focus of the jolly crowd.

'Uncle Eanraig seemed so displeased don't you think? Surely the jugglers could not have upset him so,' Juju asks.

'Perhaps a little,' I say, with a wry smile. For no doubt my uncle was indeed furious, not at the juggler's slight, but at the loss of his precious treasure that I so boldly took and placed back at Smailholm.

It pleases me so to imagine the scene, him standing in my father's chamber scratching his wrinkled brow, his mind tangled at the sudden disappearance of Mrs Jetty. Indeed, he did well to hide his displeasure at the wedding feast. Still, I could not help but notice his eyes narrowed and aimed in my direction as he talked animatedly with the king quog. Indeed, later as I took to a quiet corner and watched the merry dancing, he boldly came to sit at my side and whisper his displeasure in my ear.

What could I possibly know of pocket-sized sprites, I said. If indeed they did exist at all, like the folk tales say they do, it would be quite something for my eyes to behold and would surely make a man rich with gold.

He sat by my side, the silence between us deafening. Until he tutted, his eyes stabbing me with a baleful glare, and rose and left my side. As he disappeared into the merry crowd, I noticed Fie take Jenny's hand. A slight shake of her head and the saddest of smiles upon her lips may have told Fie that she didn't want to dance. For how could she enjoy the moment with her brother still lost? But Fie being Fie took her hand anyway and twirled her around with the jolly melody until her sad smile turned to laughter. As I felt the wetness of tears upon my cheek, I thought of another happy scene, of myself with Jimmy on the dance floor, and Vargo darting between our legs.

Later, as my sisters and Rubin were readying themselves to leave for Traquair, I made a point to bid farewell to my uncle as he solemnly moped in my father's chamber. I wished him happiness and thanked him for his effort to secure our places at Traquair, as any good niece would do. As my warm words thawed his anger I took it upon myself to place in his hand a glass of mead and proposed a toast to the success of our family. 'To happiness and success dear uncle, long may it be so,' and as I raised my glass and saw him greedily drink down the mead, I quickly turned on my heel.

'Goodbye uncle, may you find happiness in smallest of things,' I said. The irony of my farewell words did not escape me—I had laced his drink with ground quince seed, the last remaining from our journey. Of course, I knew only too well the seed would last no more than a day or two. Even so, it would give me such pleasure on my long journey to Traquair to imagine his confusion at finding himself shrunk to the smallest of sizes so unexpectedly. I wondered too if my grandmother would be looking on from the place wherein she now rested—a wry smile upon her face.

'And what of your good friends, Wynn? Father is surely indebted to such men for your return and no doubt will reward them handsomely,' says Anne, interrupting my thoughts. I smile as I think on such a question, for I think of Jenny and her arrow that saved me on more than one occasion.

''Tis such a mystery for the Falmouth name to return to these parts,' Juju says. 'Mother says it has been gone many a year, a noble family carried that name before it disappeared.'

I smile at the thought of Fie taking up residence in the lodge at Thirlestane, a gift from my father with thanks for my safe return. It will suit him well I think—land to suit his title after all these years searching. He will surely take Jenny as his bride, though I suspect such a life will not come easy to her.

Before we bade our fond goodbyes, they promised to search for Jimmy and Vargo, and plan to return to the moon folk first for guidance. So strange to part from such friends with so few words. I wondered what to say to them, for Jenny's loss was as much mine and it still weighed heavy between us. I do know though that we will all search so long as we still breathe upon this land.

'The king quog must surely realise there is no place for him at Traquair,' Anne says. 'Such a ghastly creature—I cannot bear to look at him. Goodness knows why Uncle Eanraig agreed for him to be present at the Yule feast.'

'Tis it not obvious that he paves his way with the gold he freely gives?' Rubin says.

'Well surely, he will not stay long, for I cannot imagine the reaction to the endless water that drips from his eyes, and all that snorting unknown potions is sure to offend the court,' Juju says, a distasteful grimace passing across her face.

Since arriving back at Smailholm it is true I have avoided the king, but not because his appearance offends me so, more that I worry about what other bargains he has planned.

In passing, as I left, he took my hand in his talons and whispered that he had not forgotten our own agreement—'a quog bargain is always kept'—and to enjoy the gift that he has arranged to be sent to my new chamber at Traquair. I cannot think of any gift that I would welcome that came from those twisted talons. He told me he was sorry that he couldn't travel with me to

Traquair, but that he would join soon thereafter, when business dealings with my uncle had been settled. I did not ask about Jimmy and Vargo, even though I wanted to with all my heart. Something in the pit of my stomach made me afraid of his reply.

Suddenly, the carriage bumps wildly, pushing me forward to the open window. As I steady myself on the wooden frame I take one last glimpse back at the Tower, its mighty form now dwarfed by the huge expanse of moor that separates us. As I bide a thoughtful farewell to my home, to Fie and Jenny and to the pocket-sized world of Smailholm, I turn my head to look in the other direction where the mountains grow taller and the valley weaves its way down all the way to Traquair.

TRAQUAIR

When we finally arrive at Traquair, my eyes are heavy with the want of a bed. It has been a long and tiring journey and the comforting warm orange glow of sunset bathes my face as I lean out of the carriage window. I did not realise how far such a place was from my home and I wonder how I might ever return to look upon Smailholm Tower again.

As our carriage settles to a stop, I glance up at the towering white walls of Traquair and tremble at the sheer scale of it. It is such a grand house, much bigger than I could have imagined, and dwarfs anything I have come to look upon before, including Smailholm Tower. I look upwards, counting, '10, 12, 14 windows' I say under my breath. What could one want with so many rooms?

I see six servants standing to attention at either side of a grand oak door. As Rubin steps from the carriage, offering his hand to his new wife, a short, stocky man steps forward and greets them both warmly. When the usual pleasantries have been exchanged, I too step out of the carriage to greet him, glancing upwards momentarily at the gleaming cream façade of Traquair.

'She is a fine house is she not?' he says, glancing up himself to admire it. Despite such a short stature he is a striking man of mid years, his wavy auburn hair and prominent moustache framing a youthful face, marked only by the faintest of lines around his deep blue eyes. His strongly built body is rightly shown off by the finest of blue frock coats with embossed golden buttons and tight grey trews tied at the knee.

He strokes his long moustache and twists it to a fine point between his finger and thumb. 'Please excuse me my lady, I have been most discourteous in my greeting. Let me introduce myself—I am Laird Traquair and welcome you to my home,' he says, and he bends down slightly, crossing one knee over the other and takes my hand to kiss it.

'Anne-Wynn, the middle child of the Laird Hoppringle, is it not?' he asks.

'Yes, my Laird, that is I,' I say, shyly looking away, unsure of what words should pass between us once the formality of our greeting is complete. For Uncle Eanraig's words are now ringing in my ears; Laird Traquair recently widowed, a match of marriage to tame my feisty temperament.

'Well you are all most welcome here and I look forward to speaking with you in time. Alas, I must depart on an errand of sorts. Steward, please see the ladies to their chambers?' he says curtly, summoning a servant to his side. 'I hope you find your chambers to your liking and I should be glad of your company at dinner this eve,' and with that he turns on his heel and departs swiftly back through the oak door.

'Laird Traquair, the 4th Laird and captain no less of the Queen's guard. What a fine man he is—if a little short do you not think?' Juju whispers excitedly in my ear.

'Juju, please. Such gossip is not befitting of a lady of Traquair. We need to guard our manners if we are to show our rightful place is at the Queen's side when court arrives at Traquair for her hunting expedition,' Anne says, and her look of admonishment causes Juju to blush.

Swiftly, I lift my hand to cover my mouth and prevent me laughing at the thought of my sisters not sharing in such gossip.

Regardless of the immaculate exterior, as we step inside, we are taken through a series of small dark sallow rooms where dust sprinkles the air and fading sunlight crosses from window to window. The steward makes short work of his task, steering us swiftly and silently along the walkway, passing many a closed door. Finally, we reach a turret of stone spiral steps in the same ilk as Smailholm Tower, which take us up to the upper floors. Here the walkway is lighter. The steward stops in front of one closed door and silently indicates with a raise of his arm that Juju and I should enter.

'What keeps his tongue I wonder?' Juju says as together we close the heavy door behind us. 'It's smaller than I imagined,' she says with a sigh. 'But at least there is a good view of the gardens.'

I walk towards the lead window and peer out through its glass, and so grey and cloudy is its perspective that I struggle to look upon the green land beneath. I close my eyes and try to picture the view from my chamber at the Tower—a carpet of green rugged moor with the purple heather and the brambles of Smailholm.

The garden I look upon reminds me of Abbotsford House, where father took us for merry dances at Yule. Its straight lines and formal borders crisscross and weave in uniform shapes. Whilst it looks so uniform and crisp, the further my eyes wander the more ragged it becomes. It is no wild moor I think.

'I am excited to see Anne's chamber. Will you accompany me?' Juju says, her eyes exploring the room.

'I am a little tired and must rest before dinner. You go ahead.'

'Very well,' she says, and I can tell she is disappointed at my lack of enthusiasm to explore.

As she swiftly leaves the room, I look upon the small wooden bed and long for sleep. Just as I think about burying my head in the soft pillow my eye catches a flash of light—as the low beam of sunset streams through the window. There next to my bed is a small wooden dressing table and upon it sits a gilded handheld looking glass.

I pick it up to examine its finery, for it is surely the most beautifully crafted looking glass I have ever seen. Golden leaves and rose buds weave their way around an oval glass and extend their vines all the way down its long delicate handle. As I turn it over I am perplexed to find a small note inscribed in its lead casing.

To Wynn, may you find some comfort in this gift of mine
For the quog bargain you made

It does not escape me, the strangeness of this gift from one with such an ugly reflection. How I might seek comfort in such an object eludes me, for the king quog cannot know me at all if he thinks a looking glass will ease my heartache, finely crafted though it may be.

I place it face down upon the dressing table and sink into the bed, where I pray sleep will quickly take me from my tormented thoughts.

Later, after I have taken a fitful sleep, I wake to find it is dark outside. The room is bathed in candlelight and the full moon casts its light onto the windows. I watch from my bed as Juju sings and twirls, admiring the skirt of her fine green gown as it swishes back and forth from her tiny waist—a present too from the quog king, it would appear. How much better he knows my sister's whims I think.

'Such a gown! Look it is made from the finest silk and the detail of the embroidery on my cuff is exquisite. I must thank him when he arrives. Who would have thought such a ghastly creature capable of choosing such beauty,' Juju says, her pretty face tightening into a frown as her eyes wander to my dishevelled appearance. 'Wynn you really must ready yourself, dinner is upon us and we cannot be late. I will return shortly with Anne and Rubin,' she says as she leaves the room in haste, no doubt to show our sister her new dress.

I peel my aching limbs from the bed and sit up to take stock of my appearance. As usual my hair is a befuddled mess of curls, flattened and knotted from my sleep. I pull out Deablin's black jewelled comb from my dress pocket. I have not looked upon it since leaving Rubers Law, but will use it now to pick the knots from my hair. For what other use I can make of it I do not know. I look upon the looking glass and pick it up, turning it over to reveal my ruddy cheeked reflection. Both gifts, I think, do not offer much comfort.

As I peer absentmindedly into the looking glass I realise whilst my face has grown thinner and more drawn, and perhaps a little older, my blotchy red cheeks remain. I rub my palms against them, and I notice the full moon reflect upon the glass from the window behind. So strong is its light that I can no longer gaze upon myself. Instead I am transfixed by the boldness of the moon, so full in shape for this night and speckled with hundreds of tiny stars that gather around it.

As I move my hand to touch the glass, I notice that the reflection of the moon now appears smaller. I look back at the window and then again at the looking glass, and as I do so the reflection changes and a white-cloaked figure appears within the glass.

'A moon creature!' I cry out loud, for so surprising

is the vision, I do not believe what my eyes see. How could it be so? As clearly as my reflection once was, so is the reflection of the white-cloaked moon creature now peering back at me.

There are no words that pass between us, just as when he kneeled beside me and took my hand in Moon Coppice. Instead he nods his hooded face and steps backwards, wherein his draped arm appears in view and points to the very place where I had first met him—the centre of the coppice, a grassy mound encircling a shallow trough.

As the water in the trough appears fully in the glass its water ripples then settles into perfect stillness. There in its black water I see a vision bathed in light. A story of light emerging—of the quog king ordering a search of Rubers Law for Jimmy and Vargo. Their lifeless bodies found in the furthest, darkest corner of its great belly. Finally, a journey that takes them by carriage, their bodies lain perfectly still, through a great forest. And beyond across a purple plain to a small coppice of twelve tightly knitted trees. There the story in the water ends and a moon creature appears once more to face me directly in the glass. Sensing my curiosity to see more, he steps backwards to reveal the tranquil scene behind him. There beside the trough are two small figures—a man, dressed in a dark hooded cape, and that of a dog, golden in the shine of the moonlight. As my view clears I see the man pull down his hood to reveal a wave of white blond hair.

'Jimmy, Vargo!' I shout, trembling with happiness at

229

the vision in the water. Can it be real? So troublesome my mind now seems. So difficult it is to work out what is real and what is not. It does appear the king has kept his bargain—and perhaps I have been unkind. For he is surely not a creature to be feared when he has helped me find those lost to me, even if the vision before me is so strange.

But what of the price that my grandmother spoke of? Perhaps like she, I now see things that others don't. The spirits of Rubers Law still weigh heavy on my mind. Will her fate now be mine? Am I capable too of using such magic in wrath upon another? For surely, to know such a gift is the price itself. I know that gift is no longer welcomed in this world. It causes fear to rip through the heart of many a man. Surely, they will not hesitate to banish me, as they did Deablin, to Rubers Law. Or worse still, hang me from the gallows, carrying with me the name of witch.

At such a realisation, my hand slips from the handle and the looking glass drops into my lap. I quickly pick it up and the reflection that greets me now is that of my own and I cry, a deep hollow cry that only a wounded animal in the deep of night might give. I look back out of the window and I find that the moon is now hidden in the clouds.

'I will see you again my dearest friends,' I say.

'for a quog bargain is always kept.'

HISTORICAL NOTE

Many of the places in this book exist. Smailholm Tower is a real peel tower, around 5 miles west of Kelso in the Scottish Borders in Great Britain. It was originally built in the 15th century by the Hoppringle family to protect occupants from sporadic English raids. The family held the lands of Smailholm from the early 15th century and managed part of Ettrick Forest for their feudal superior the Earl of Douglas. The Tower provided the inspiration to Sir Walter Scott, who visited his paternal grandfather here when still a boy. Smailholm provides the setting for Scott's ballad The Eve of St John. The name Smailholm can be translated from Old English to read small little island. Ettrick Forest, Traquair and Rubers Law also exist. At the summit of Rubers Law is a volcanic vent that was formed roughly 330 million years ago.

All the characters in this book are fictional, apart from the references to Mary Queen of Scots, who really did visit Traquair in 1566. The story of the three Annes is loosely based on the Lament of Queen Marie. Mary Queen of Scots had four waiting women all of the name Mary.

Yestreen the queen had four Maries. The night she'll hae but three;

There was Marie Seton and Marie Beaton,
And Marie Carmichael
and me.

The Golden Retriever was originally bred in Scotland, but not until the mid-19th century. The belief in diminutive beings such as sprites, elves and fairies is common place in Scottish folklore. During the late 1500s there was great mistrust around the practice of witchcraft. In the period between 1590 and 1700, some 3,837 individuals in Scotland were tried as witches, many of them women. Of these, 205 were executed.

ACKNOWLEDGEMENTS

The love, support and enthusiasm from my husband Howard has made this book possible. To my children Ava and Henry—your undoubting belief in magic inspired me every day to put pen to paper.

To my family and friends, you know who you are. Thank you for believing in me, even when I didn't believe in myself. Special thanks must go to my friend David Rolls, an incredibly talented artist who provided the illustrations for this book. You've supported me over the years on endless mad cap schemes. Finally one actually happened.

To my editor Gary Dalkin for providing the most sensible advice and steering me through the uncharted territory of writing my first novel. To Holly Dunn and Joshua Stolarz—exceptional talents in book cover and map design respectively. Even though we were all thousands of miles apart and different time zones you made the process a breeze.

ABOUT THE AUTHOR

Claire Williams lives in Cheshire with her husband and children Ava and Henry. She is proud to be called a 'Clayhead'—a person born in the Potteries (Stoke on Trent) and will always turn over a china cup to see where it is made. She is a huge fantasy fan and will often be found snuggled in front of the TV watching a sci-fi or fantasy movie. *Smailholm* is her first novel, inspired by visits to the Scottish Borders on family holidays.

TRAQUAIR

Book Two

Coming Soon
For updates visit
www.clwilliamsauthor.com

Or scan the code with your phone camera to visit the
author's website.

FREE 𝔖mailholm GAME